Dragos Takes a Holiday

Thea Harrison

Dragos Takes a Holiday
Copyright © 2013 by Teddy Harrison LLC
ISBN 13: 978-0-9899728-1-9
Print Edition

This book is a work of fiction. The names, characters, places, and incidents are products of the writer's imagination or have been used fictitiously and are not to be construed as real. Any resemblance to persons, living or dead, actual events, locale or organizations is entirely coincidental.

The Bermuda Triangle. Pirates. The Peanut. What could possibly go wrong?

Dragos Cuelebre needs a vacation. So does Pia, his mate. When the First Family of the Wyr head to Bermuda for some much needed R&R, it's no ordinary undertaking – and no ordinary weekend in the sun. Between hunting for ancient treasure buried beneath the waves and keeping track of their son, Liam—a.k.a. Peanut, whose Wyr abilities are manifesting far ahead of schedule—it's a miracle that Pia and Dragos can get any time together.

They're determined to make the most of each moment, no matter who tries to get in their way.

And did we mention pirates?

For fans of DRAGON BOUND and LORD'S FALL, passion, playfulness, and adventure abound in this Elder Races novella.

Chapter One

O ne evening after a particularly brutal day at work, Dragos leaned against the refrigerator and watched Pia cook dinner.

They had personal chefs. They could order takeout from any restaurant in New York, but these days, more often than not, Pia chose to cook. Although she was a lifelong dedicated vegan, she had overcome her revulsion for handling meat for his sake. He loved to watch her pore over recipes with her tongue between her teeth, and he enjoyed every meal she cooked for him, which she often set in front of him with an air of triumph and relief.

After preparing a sirloin roast with carrots and potatoes in one pan, she placed a strange-looking lump in a smaller, separate pan and set vegetables around that too.

Dragos asked, "What on earth is that?"

"It's a vegan harvest roast."

He shook his head. "I'm sorry, lover, someone should have taught you this by now. The words 'vegan' and 'roast' do not go together in the same sentence." He eyed the unappetizing lump with skepticism. "What's it made of?"

Pia glanced at him, amused. "Seitan, different kinds of flour, seeds, soy sauce, seasonings, sometimes nuts…"

He lost interest after the first ingredient. "In other words, nothing edible."

"You might not think it's edible, but I think it's delicious." She wiped her hands on a towel and gave him a cheerful grin. "You're welcome to try it after it's cooked."

He grinned back. "No thanks, I'll pass."

His grin faded again almost immediately. He'd had a bitch of a day, but every workday was a bitch these days. It had started last year when Dragos had lost two of his seven sentinels to mating with women who lived outside the Wyr demesne.

This year had not gone any easier. He had finally replaced Rune and Tiago with two new sentinels, but now all the older sentinels needed vacations. As Dragos's First, Graydon had insisted on going last. By the time Graydon came back from his vacation, Dragos would have been operating short-staffed for more than a year.

Dragos had a short temper at the best of times. Now he was liable to bite somebody's head off if they looked at him funny.

For now, he was glad the day was over. He leaned back against the kitchen counter, still wearing the suit he had put on for work at six thirty that morning.

Liam had awakened from his nap, and Dragos held him against his shoulder. Even though the baby was three months old, he was growing at an inhumanly quick rate and exhibiting abilities far beyond most babies his age. At his last checkup, Pia's physician, Dr. Medina, said he had grown twice the size of a three-month-old human baby.

He could already sit up easily. A few days ago, he had gotten to his hands and knees and rocked. Soon he would be crawling, and he understood far more of what people said than most realized. He was the first ever dragon child, and he was so full of magic his small body glowed with it. Nobody knew what to expect from him, not even Dragos.

Both father and son watched Pia move around the kitchen. She had used a hot iron and pinned up her hair so that it fell in loose, soft curls of pale gold. Dragos itched to sink his hands into the shining, luxurious mass.

Post pregnancy, her body had returned to its slim runner's build, except now her breasts and her hips were slightly fuller. After the first month or so of startled indecision, she had taken to wearing form fitting clothing that accentuated her new curves and drove Dragos wild.

Tonight she wore a saucy red-and-white halter dress with a tucked-in waist and a flaring, knee-length skirt. Large strawberries splashed bright circles of red on the soft material, accented with a touch of green at the stem. She had painted her toes the same shade of cheerful red and walked around the kitchen barefoot, and Dragos wanted to eat her all up.

Later, he promised himself. After they put Liam to bed, and the penthouse was shadowed and quiet, Dragos would carry Pia out to the terrace, lay her down on one of the cushioned lounge chairs underneath the stars, and feast on every inch of her delectable body. He would raise that sexy skirt of hers and ease her gorgeous legs apart…

Liam fussed and knuckled his round little face. Dragos considered the baby with a frown. Normally Liam had a sunny disposition. It was unlike him to be so fussy. His silky tufts of white-blond hair wafted in the air around his head, and his dark violet eyes looked puffy and tired.

Pia opened the convection-oven door, set in the two roast pans and glanced at Liam too. "I think he's already teething. He's had a tough couple of days. He keeps wanting to nurse, and today he's been fussing and rubbing his face. When I coaxed him to open his mouth earlier, I could see white lines at his gums."

"Good." Dragos patted Liam's diapered bottom gently. "A dragon needs a healthy set of teeth."

Pia widened her eyes at him and grinned. "Yes, of course he needs them, but he's only three months old!"

He shrugged. "He's got quite a bit of growing to do, and he's going to need a lot of meat. It's possible his dragon form will end up as big as mine."

"He's not developing so much as he's exploding into reality." Pia shook his head. "I guess he's creating his own definition of normal. We just have to figure out a way to keep up with him."

Dragos smiled at her over the baby's head. "We defeated the Dark Fae King. We can cope with one precocious child."

"You always sound so confident." She walked over to the stainless-steel island where a bottle of red wine stood alongside two wineglasses. Dragos noted with pleasure that she had opened one of his favorites, a Chateau Lafite Rothschild Pauillac that had once in Versailles been dubbed "the King's wine."

"That's because I am confident."

"No doubt you're right." She concentrated on pouring the rich ruby liquid into the glasses. "I think his bunny is in the living room. It might make him feel better. Would you mind getting it?"

"Of course." He took the baby down the hall.

Liam's bunny was one of those things Dragos didn't understand. The stuffed toy was floppy, super soft and had big, dark eyes. Liam adored it, although Dragos wasn't quite sure why. In real life, a bunny that size would barely make an appetizer.

His iPhone buzzed in his suit pocket. He checked it. Graydon's name lit up the display. He could leave a message. Dragos pressed the ignore button as he scanned the living room. Most of the spacious area lay in shadows, but a few accent lights remained on. Liam's bunny lay on one end of the couch. As he strode over to it, a flash of gold caught his eye.

He turned, his attention sharpening.

The flash of gold came from the front jacket of a hardcover book. It sat atop a pile of several books on one of the end tables. Absently, Dragos scooped up the soft toy and presented it to Liam. Liam snatched at the bunny and hugged it while he laid his head on Dragos's chest. Dragos cupped the back of the baby's soft head, cuddling him, as he strolled over to get a proper look at the cover.

The book was lavishly decorated in rich, eye-catching colors. A treasure chest sat on a bronze background, underneath the title *Missing Treasures of the Seventeenth Century*. Old, gold doubloons spilled out of the open lid.

Dragos flipped open the book. It was from the public library. He read the inside of the jacket. The narrative focused on several European ships that had gone missing on voyages of exploration.

Pia walked into the living room carrying two glasses of wine. He said, "I don't know why you keep going to the library instead of buying any book that you want."

"Because going to the library is an experience." Pia set his glass on the end table and curled up at one end of the couch. "It's a fun outing away from the Tower, Liam enjoys story time and the other babies, and I like supporting the library."

While she talked, he made a mental note to write a large check for the public library system. If Pia and Liam enjoyed going, he would make sure the library could provide them with anything they wanted.

"Why don't I have this book?" He owned several books about treasure in his own personal library, but he knew he didn't have this one. He would have remembered the flashy gold cover.

"You've been pretty busy. It came out last November."

"Mm."

He set it aside and picked up the next one, a large, trade-sized paperback entitled *The Lost Elders*. This one was decorated with a heavy, glossed cover. He flipped it over to scan the blurb on the back.

"I don't have this one either." He frowned.

"I think that one came out in March. I've skimmed all your books about treasure, and they made me curious, so I only checked out books that you don't already have." Pia sipped her wine. "Didn't you say that you used to hunt for lost treasure?"

"Yes, I did. Of course, I had a lot more free time in those days." He hefted the paperback in one hand as his gaze went unfocused. "I remember when this happened."

"Really?"

"It was early in the fifteenth century. Isabeau, the Light Fae Queen in Ireland, and her younger twin sister, Tatiana, had been feuding for several years. Tatiana sent the ship *Sebille* to scout for a new land where she could settle with her followers. The ship was rumored to have been loaded with gold and all kinds of treasure, so that the captain could negotiate with indigenous people for land rights."

"Tatiana… Do you mean the Light Fae Queen in Los Angeles?" Pia asked.

"Yes." He set the book down and settled beside her on the couch. Liam had started to chew on one of the bunny's floppy ears. "Eventually she settled in southern California, but the *Sebille* disappeared completely, and people have been looking for it ever since. Some even said that Isabeau caught wind of the expedition and sabotaged it, but I doubt that. From everything I've heard, Isabeau wanted to get rid of Tatiana as much as Tatiana wanted to leave."

Pia slid close to him and rested her head on his shoulder. Warmth filled him, and he put an arm around her as she rubbed Liam's back. "What do you suppose happened to the *Sebille*?"

Dragos thought back. "There were rumors that it sank off the southeastern coast of North America. I wonder if this book goes into more detail."

She lifted her head. "You mean it might have gotten lost somewhere around the Bermuda Triangle?"

"It's possible, although back then it wasn't called the Bermuda Triangle." Unwilling to reach for his glass and disturb either Pia or Liam, he took a sip from her wineglass and handed it back to her. "It was called the Devil's Triangle, and still is sometimes. The area wasn't very well understood at the time the ship went missing."

"I didn't know it was that well understood now."

He gave into temptation and sank his hand into her soft, luxuriant hair. "It's unpredictable, which is not quite the same thing. There's a tangle of crossover passageways all over the area. The routes loop around and over each other, and the shifting ocean currents make most of them virtually impossible to map, although some old legends say that pirates found passageways to Other lands where they lived in secret hideouts."

She shuddered. "You could get caught up in one of those passageways and get lost forever."

"Yes, theoretically, and it's possible that the *Sebille* did just that." He tilted his head and buried his face in her hair, which was soft like silk and scented with her floral shampoo. "But it's also not likely, either, because they would have needed to stumble onto the exact path of the crossover passageway. If ships stick to the established shipping lanes, they're safe enough. Probably the *Sebille* sank."

"Have you been to Bermuda?" She walked her fingers across his chest.

"No, I've only flown over it several times."

"Bermuda, the Bahamas, the Caribbean—I've never been anywhere like that. I bet they're beautiful." She sounded wistful.

His phone buzzed, and they both sighed. He pulled the phone out of his jacket pocket and checked the display. It was Graydon again. Dragos gritted his teeth. "How long before we eat?"

They had come to a mutual decision several months ago. Dragos would not take any business or sentinel calls during dinner. Pia told him, "We've got at least a half an hour. You have time to take the call."

He kissed her forehead, handed Liam over to her, and stood to walk down the hallway as he answered his phone.

"Sorry to bother you." Graydon always apologized when he called after work hours.

"Never mind, what is it?" Dragos asked.

After listening to a few sentences, he switched direction and walked back into the living room. He met Pia's gaze. "Would you mind keeping dinner warm for me? I'll be as quick as I can."

She nodded, looking unsurprised. "Of course."

He strode out and didn't make it back until after midnight.

When he finally returned home, the penthouse lay in deep shadow, except for the kitchen, where a light burned over the stove. Pia had left a note on the counter. *Your supper plate is in the fridge. Microwave for three minutes. Love you.*

He smiled. She had never lost patience, no matter how challenging this last year had become. He opened the fridge to locate his supper. She had plated the roast-beef meal beautifully and even garnished it with a sprig of parsley.

Too hungry to wait while the food heated, he ate it cold, standing at the counter. Looking forward to sliding between cool silk sheets, he walked down the hall to the heart of the place, the large bedroom he shared with Pia.

She had left another light on, her bedside lamp. Wearing dark blue cotton shorts and a thin, matching T-shirt with spaghetti straps, she had tucked her legs underneath the covers and sprawled across the bed on her stomach, fast asleep. The pile of library books lay strewn around her like abandoned toys. The fingers of her right hand curled around *The Lost Elders*.

Moving gently so he didn't wake her, he stacked the library books on her nightstand. As he leaned to pick up *The Lost Elders*, the sound of Liam crying came over the baby monitor.

Pia stirred. "Unh."

"Stay where you are," Dragos whispered. "I'll take care of him."

"You sure?" Her voice was sleep blurred. "You've had such a long day."

"I'm positive."

"Is everything okay?"

"Everything is fine. Go back to sleep."

He pressed a kiss to her bare shoulder, pulled the bedcovers up and tucked them around her. Still carrying the book, he walked into the nursery.

The mellow glow from a nightlight lit the room. In the crib, Liam had come up on his hands and knees but sank back a bit, so that he sat like a frog as he cried. Dragos set the book on the side table by the rocking chair and gathered up the baby.

"What is this?" He kept his voice soft and gentle. "Life is not nearly half as tragic as you think it is."

Liam shuddered and hiccupped, blinking up at Dragos with violet eyes that swam with tears. He embodied innocence, his energy so bright, shining and new, and Dragos loved him with a ferocity he had never felt about anything or anyone before, except for Pia.

"Now, what's wrong?" Dragos asked. "Is it your mouth?"

The baby nodded, and his soft face crumpled.

He nestled Liam against his chest. "I'll make it better."

He walked to the large rocking chair, sat and whispered a beguilement until Liam's small body relaxed. The baby sucked his thumb for a while and fell asleep as Dragos rocked him.

Peace settled around Dragos like a warm blanket. He was tired, and he wanted to go to bed. He wanted to block out the rest of the world and make love to Pia. But this quiet, intimate time with his son was too perfect, and it would pass all too soon. He would not be too quick to turn away from moments like this.

He remembered the book and picked it up. Still rocking, Dragos opened it. He began to read, and lost himself in thoughts of ancient gold and lost treasure.

Chapter Two

"You sure you weren't too clever for him?" Eva asked. "Don't get me wrong, I know he's bright. He's Lord of the Wyr and all, but he *is* still just a man."

Despite Eva's skepticism, Pia remained unfazed. "Wait and see. It isn't a matter of 'if' we go on vacation. It's a matter of 'when.'"

Bright morning sunlight streamed into Dragos and Pia's bedroom, although calling it a bedroom was a bit of a misnomer. The room was massive, with the king-sized bed at one end, and a fireplace and white couches at the other end. When Pia had come to live in Cuelebre Tower, the room had been stark, but she had added bright patches of color with jewel-toned pillows and throws, a rich bedspread and rugs.

Pia stood beside the bed where she had piled things to pack. She swung her suitcase up and opened it.

Eva lay sprawled on the floor in front of the French doors with a thick, soft blanket spread out beside her for Liam to play on. Not that Eva was having a great deal of success keeping Liam on the blanket. He had started another new thing that morning. He was busily scooting backwards everywhere.

"You're so sure, you're already packing?"

"Yes. He needs a break, and he wants it. He just might not know it yet. He's so tired he fell asleep in the nursery last night when he was rocking the peanut. That's where I found them both this morning." She looked at Eva pointedly. "*Dragos* fell asleep. Normally he can stay awake for days if he needs to."

Eva scratched the back of her head. The sunlight gleamed gold on her dark brown skin. "I just hope you aren't counting your chickens before they're hatched."

"Mark my words, you should pack too." Pia wagged her finger at the other woman. "He's remarkably decisive when he makes his mind up about something. We could be on the plane as soon as tomorrow, or even tonight. I'm going to suggest that we only take you and Hugh with us."

Eva sat up straight. "Sweet."

Pia paused to watch Liam scoot backwards toward her, his little diapered butt in the air, and barely managed to keep from laughing out loud. He was sharp as a whip, and he might figure out she was laughing at him. She didn't want to hurt his feelings.

She told Eva, "We won't need bodyguards, but I do want to have babysitters so Dragos and I can go out by ourselves."

"I'll take it." Eva grinned. "Do we by any chance know where Dragos will want to go on vacation?"

Pia scowled. "No, of course not. But I wouldn't rule out Bermuda, the Caribbean, or Cape Horn."

Eva cocked her head. "Am I sensing a water theme?"

"You're sensing a shipwreck theme." Pia shook out a skirt and carefully folded it. "Or maybe I should say a theme about lost treasure."

"You're talking about those books you got from the library the other day, aren't you? Dayum, you're good. Does Graydon know we're leaving?"

Pia blinked at her. "Know what? Nothing's been decided yet."

Eva laughed and rolled to her feet. "I'll go tell Hugh and pack."

As Eva left, Pia checked her toiletries bag. It was filled with miniature bottles of everything she would need. She set it in her suitcase and bent to pick up the Peanut.

She whispered, "We have to pack for you too, you know. I'm guessing we might be going to Bermuda, since your daddy read that whole book in the middle of the night."

The baby looked deep into her eyes and patted her face.

Mommy carried him into his room. He thought things were going well until she set him on the thick, soft rug in the middle of the floor.

No, that wasn't what he wanted. That was very much not what he wanted.

He was tired again, and his mouth hurt, and he was hungry all the time. Hungry for what, he didn't know. Hungry, hungry.

So he scowled and concentrated mightily on *something that he wanted.*

And the world shifted.

He felt better. Quite a bit better, actually. His new mouth didn't hurt at all, but he was still very hungry.

Mommy kept talking as she moved around his room. She pulled diapers out of drawers, set them on the changing table and turned to the closet. "…I want to take you to the beach and play in the sand with you, except I don't know that we should. Are you too young to play in sand, or to go into salt water? Peanut, you are such a statistical outlier, half the time I have no idea what we should do with you."

She turned away from the closet, her arms full of clothes. When she looked at him, she shrieked and dropped everything.

It startled him so badly he felt a burst of anxiety. He turned around to scoot backward toward her as fast as he could, but something flopped along his back, and his arms and legs weren't quite working the way they should. He stopped, confused, and stared down at himself.

Slender white forelegs stretched to the floor. He raised a front paw, staring at the strange talons. His back felt odd too, and he looked over his shoulder, flexing sleek, graceful wings. A tail trailed the floor behind him. He reached for it with one forepaw, tugged the end and his butt wagged. The tail was attached to him.

Mommy knelt in front of him and cupped his face. He looked up into her eyes. She had grown teary, and yet she was smiling. "You are the cleverest baby ever. You're so beautiful, and exactly how I first dreamed of you."

Pleasure washed over him, and he smiled at her.

Her eyes went very round. She beamed at him. "That's quite a mouthful of toofers you've got there, too."

She gathered him up in her arms. He tucked his snout into the crook of her neck, and it was so good, almost everything he wanted, except…

He was *so* hungry.

He fussed and whined, and she sat on the floor and rocked him, while she dug her cell phone out of her pocket and moved her thumb rapidly over the keypad. "Dragos, you have to come home right now."

Daddy's sharp voice came over the phone. "What's wrong?"

"Nothing's wrong exactly, but Liam has changed and he's upset."

"What do you mean, he's changed?"

The pace of Mommy's rocking picked up, but she spoke softly. "I mean he's in his dragon form, and I can't tell you how beautiful he is. He's also upset for some reason. Maybe it scared him? And you're missing all of it. You need to come see this."

"I'll be right there."

Mommy set the phone aside as Liam whined and plucked at her shirt. "Are you hungry?" she asked gently. He nodded. "I can't nurse you when you're like this, sweetheart, not with all of those razor-sharp teeth."

That was the saddest thing he had ever heard in his whole life. He lifted his head and looked at her, grief stricken.

"Oh, Peanut, I'm so sorry. Please don't look at me that way." They considered each other desperately. Mommy's expression turned firm. He folded his wings back and clung to her as she rolled to her feet and carried him to the kitchen.

She opened the fridge door and pulled out a pan that had the something he was craving. It smelled oh so good. His stomach rumbled and he arched toward it, reaching with both front paws.

"Hold on—let me get the plastic wrap off first."

As she slid to the floor, he struggled to get to the appetizing smell. She snatched off the plastic wrap, set the pan on the kitchen tile, and he fell on the leftover sirloin roast. Eyes closed, his whole body tense, he focused on gorging on the meat.

Running footsteps sounded in the background, but it was only Daddy, so he ignored it. A moment later, Daddy said in a quiet voice, "Well, damn. Look at that. Hello, little man."

A large, gentle hand came down on Liam's back, between his wings, and contentment filled him.

"I didn't know what else to do." She gestured to the pan. "He acted like he was starving, and he has all those teeth. Then I remembered what you said about how he was going to need a lot of meat."

"He gave you clues about what he needed, and you followed your instincts," said Daddy. "You did exactly what you should have done."

Liam finished off the roast. The hungriness had gone away, and his belly felt comfortably stretched and full. Sleepiness descended. Eyes drooping, he looked over his shoulder. Daddy and Mommy knelt on either side of him, both smiling.

He scooted backward toward Mommy. When she gathered him up, he turned to climb up her body until he lay draped along her shoulders.

"I'm telling you, this is just like my dreams." Mommy reached up to stroke his leg. He stopped listening to their conversation, tucked his snout in the neckline of her shirt and fell fast asleep.

Relief had turned her leg muscles into noodles, so Pia shifted to sit on the floor, and Dragos joined her. He leaned back against the fridge while she sat forward with her spine straight. She didn't want to disturb Liam while he was resting on her.

She angled her head and looked at Dragos. "What are we going to do if he doesn't change back into human form, and he keeps growing at this rate?"

He stretched his legs out, loosened his tie and scratched his jaw. Even though it was just midday, a new growth of beard shadowed his lean cheeks. He kept his inky-black hair cut uncompromisingly short, and the formality of his dark suit highlighted the richness of his copper skin and intelligent, gold eyes.

In the last year, Pia had gone from living at the edge of Wyr society to being catapulted directly to the top. She had met any number of Powerful creatures in the different Elder Races from all over the world, but none of them, to her mind, had Dragos's sheer physicality. Standing just under seven feet tall and weighing close to three hundred pounds, he towered over the largest of his sentinels, and his dragon form was the size of a Cessna jet.

His handsomeness had a brutality that never failed to cause her breath to catch at the back of her throat. Not even tiredness could dim the Power and energy that boiled from him. He was as strong as the earth, and whenever she laid eyes on him she felt her soul winging out of her body, arrowing straight toward him.

He sighed. "I should be able to coax him back into his human form, but I don't think he'll be able to stay that way. His human form has no capacity to eat meat. If he follows the pattern of other Wyr children with large animal forms, he'll need to shift back periodically to his dragon form in order to feed."

"We're going to need a bigger skyscraper." She rubbed her eyes with a thumb and forefinger. "Part of me can't believe I just said that."

Dragos's cell phone buzzed. His gold gaze flashed with irritation. Without glancing at the screen, he thumbed the phone on and said into it, "No." After he hung up, he looked at her, his expression turning rueful. "I think it's time we talk again about moving up north."

Resigned, she nodded. Dragos owned a country estate just outside of Carthage, in northern New York. Well technically, since they were married now and nobody had breathed a word to her about a prenup, she supposed she was part owner, too. The mansion had fifty rooms, a separate house for an estate manager, and it was surrounded by two hundred and fifty acres of rolling, forested hills.

They had gone to the estate for their honeymoon and had stayed in the estate manager's house, which had four bedrooms, four bathrooms and a family room with a fireplace that overlooked a lake. She loved that house. She had given birth to Liam in that house. She didn't feel any affinity whatsoever for the palatial mansion.

Still, she knew she wasn't being entirely rational. Just the sheer size of the place had intimidated her when she first saw it, but she might like it more if she spent some time there. After all, she had once felt funny about Cuelebre Tower and the penthouse, and familiarity had gone a long way to making her comfortable here.

She sighed. "He's going to need the space, isn't he? Especially when he learns to fly."

"Yes, he will. The place up north is more private, with lots of greenery and open space." He paused thoughtfully. "We can make it more secure too."

"Two hundred and fifty acres would be a hell of a backyard for him to play in," she murmured.

Pia had always followed her mother's advice and stayed in the city, which was densely populated and easier to hide in. She had never seriously considered moving to the country, but now as she poked at the idea, she realized that two hundred and fifty acres would be a hell of a backyard for her to play in too, and her Wyr form approved. It approved most strenuously.

"We can get to the city in a couple of hours if we fly in." Dragos angled his head, considering it. "That's not so bad. When you're stuck in traffic here, it can take a couple of hours just to get across town. I could have a complete office complex built on the property."

She put a hand on his leg. His hand sewn Armani suit was made of lightweight woven wool that stretched taut over the thick, powerful muscle of his thigh. "We would need more than just the office complex. There will need to be living space for security and staff, and for the sentinels, because they'll be flying back and forth. As spacious as that mansion is, it's no Cuelebre Tower. We can't all live there, nor would I want to try."

He rubbed her back, his clever fingers following the curve and hollow of her spine. "We could build along the lake. There's plenty of space to spread out. None of us would need to feel crowded."

She broached another subject hesitantly. "I would want to redecorate the main house. Maybe even do some renovations."

"You should," he told her, smiling. "Hell, you can bulldoze the place if you want, and start over from scratch."

That thought was a little too overwhelming. "I don't know if we need to go quite that far."

Dragos stroked a loose strand of hair away from her face. "But do we both believe that we need to make the move?"

She looked down. The weight of Liam's body lay draped along the back of her neck and shoulders, and his slender, graceful white legs and tail curled around her, just underneath her collarbones. While it seemed like it might be an awkward position, he didn't appear to mind at all. In fact he seemed perfectly comfortable, and he was sound asleep.

He was not a perfect white, but more of an ivory hue. His hide had the same iridescent sheen that Dragos's did, but he had gotten his pale coloring from her. She wondered what people would think when they saw him. She put a hand lightly on one of his forelegs, and he stretched, flexing his paws, and sighed.

"Yes, we need to move. But we won't have time to start building or redecorating until July. First we've got to get through all of the inter-demesne functions surrounding the summer solstice, and Graydon needs his vacation."

"Agreed." He gave her a lopsided smile that eased his harsh features and banished the tiredness from his expression. "In the meantime, is it too much upheaval if we consider taking a long weekend away?"

She loved him so much, with all of her heart. She loved his harsh side and needed his ruthlessness, because she knew he would always provide for her and Liam, and protect them with every ounce of his considerable power. But when he smiled at her like that, everything inside of her brightened, until she felt like she floated in a sea of light, and she grew weightless and dizzy with delight.

She peeked at him between her lashes. "I don't know, Dragos, this is awfully sudden. Where would you want to go?"

He tugged at a strand of her hair behind her ear, and her gaze fell to his wrist. It had been a year since she had sewn a lock of her braided hair around his wrist, and he still wore it. He had done something to protect it, and it shone with an extra sparkle of Power.

"You said you've never been to Bermuda or the Caribbean." He angled his head, watching her expression. "How would you like to go there? I think it would be fun to do some treasure hunting. We can go swimming and soak up some sunshine, and go out to eat. I could use a break before we plunge into all of the summer solstice activities, even if it's a short one, and I'll bet you could too."

She smiled. "I would really love to get away."

"How soon could you be ready to go?"

She tilted her head, and her smile turned into a grin. "Is fifteen minutes soon enough?"

"Really. Fifteen minutes." His gold eyes narrowed suddenly. "Those books. That conversation. You little Machiavellian, you set me up."

She closed one eye and held her thumb and forefinger close together. "Maybe a teensy, weensy bit. Actually, I just presented you with opportunities."

He laughed. "Is that what you call it? I should know by now to expect this kind of thing from the thief who stole from my hoard."

Her eyes rounded. "You're never going to get over it, are you? I only stole one time, and it was just a penny!"

"I can't tell you how glad I am of that," said Dragos. "Because you're pretty lousy at it. The gods only know what kind of trouble you would have gotten yourself into, if you had kept up your life of crime."

Her tone of voice turned aggrieved. "That is completely untrue. I was absolutely excellent at stealing *the very one time* I did it. I was not quite so excellent at the getaway."

"You have a point," he admitted.

She grew serious. "While everybody else has a vacation scheduled, you need and deserve a break more than anybody. But you're so driven, I knew you would have a hard time disconnecting from work unless you had something else to focus on, so I went to the library to do some research. When I found new books about ships that had disappeared, I thought if I could interest you in some treasure hunting, it would be a good way for you to stop and smell the roses—or, in your case, search for some shiny sparklies."

His eyes flashed with an acquisitive gleam. "It's been a long time since I've found a good stash of treasure."

"I know."

"And you are wiser and far kinder than I deserve," he said quietly. He leaned forward to kiss her. Her eyelids fluttered shut as his warm, hard lips caressed hers. "And so damn sneaky."

"That's one of the things you love best about me," she reminded him.

His whisper turned into a low growl. "Damn right."

"What do you have to do to get ready to leave?" She stroked his face.

"Pack. I've already talked to Graydon, and he's good with us leaving. The jet is in the hangar, so I just need to make a phone call. While we're getting ready, I'll have Kris find us a good place to stay. What about you?"

"I need to finish packing Liam's stuff, but that won't take more than five or ten minutes. I would like to take Hugh and Eva so they can babysit."

He cocked his head. "We'll go out to dinner somewhere by the beach."

She beamed at him. "You mean we'll go on a date?"

He smiled. "Just as soon as we can get out of here."

Chapter Three

S ince Liam restricted her movements, Dragos helped her pack the baby's things. While he changed out of his suit into khaki pants and a black knit shirt and packed, she called Eva and Hugh.

Eva laughed. "Girl, you got some scary mojo."

"I just know my husband." Pia felt too excited to be smug.

Eva and Hugh soon showed up at the penthouse.

They stared in shocked silence at the sleeping baby dragon draped around Pia's neck. Pia smiled as she held a finger to her lips and silently warned them to be quiet. Nodding and grinning broadly, they took charge of the luggage.

Dragos made phone calls, while Pia raided his supply of organic beef jerky in the kitchen. She wanted to have lots of snacks in her purse, in case Liam woke with the same kind of desperate hunger as he'd shown earlier.

Dragos strode into the kitchen and looked at her and Liam. "If people caught sight of him in his Wyr form, it would start a riot, and we would never get out of here. Let's take the private elevator down to the parking garage."

"Sounds good to me," she said with relief.

Liam never stirred as they rode down the elevator or climbed into the waiting limo with Eva and Hugh. Pia eased him off her shoulders and into the car seat, and after some finagling managed to get him strapped in. During the ride to the airport they talked in quiet voices. Dragos's phone buzzed, and Pia twitched. He wasn't going to get much of a break if he kept answering phone calls and text messages.

He checked the screen of his iPhone and smiled. "Kris found us a place to stay. It's a house on Cambridge Beach Bay."

He handed the phone to Pia, and she scrolled through the images. The rental was a historic, peach-colored villa with a veranda that faced the ocean, and it had eight bedrooms and five baths, private gardens and a barbeque pit. Two grocery stores were a five minutes' walk away, and restaurants, shops, and boat rentals were all in close proximity. Even better, it had a terraced path to the beach framed by flowering bushes and palm trees.

She caught a glimpse of the astronomical price tag on the webpage. The cost for renting the villa for a week was close to ten thousand dollars.

The number danced in front of her eyes. She took a deep breath and let it out slowly. There was no need to hyperventilate. Dragos deposited twice that amount each month into a personal account for her, just for incidentals. She bought herself and Peanut anything she wanted, and she still had serious money left over, enough to dump into a fast-growing, hefty savings account. The point was, they could easily afford the rental.

"Forget about me," she told Eva. "Dragos's assistant has some serious mojo." She turned to Dragos. "This is amazing. How did he get it at such short notice?"

A smile tugged at the corners of his lips. "Kris implied there was a last-minute cancellation."

Or Dragos paid the other vacationers to change their plans. She paused to listen to her internal radar. Did she feel funny about that?

Nope. Her internal radar felt quite serene today. The others would have gotten a deal they couldn't refuse, and Dragos got to take a much-needed break. Plus, beach! The water looked so lovely.

Dragos continued. "We've got the house for up to a week if we want it. The manager of the property will stock the fridge with plenty of food and drinks, and is setting up a crib for the length of our stay. We don't have to do anything when we arrive. We can just relax and do whatever we want."

Absorbed in looking at the photos, she said, "What I want to know is, why don't we have a private island?"

She had meant to be facetious, but Dragos's expression turned thoughtful. "Good question. I'll have to look into that."

Her head snapped up, and she stared at him with wide eyes. He gave her a completely serious look in return. Wordless, she faced forward.

Hugh's shoulders shook, and Eva snickered into her hand.

Dragos gently eased his phone out of her lax hands. She watched him sidelong as he turned it off.

✧   ✧   ✧

The flight was short, just over two hours long. Eva and Hugh sat at the front of the cabin, talking and playing chess. Dragos and Pia settled with Liam on one of the two couches toward the back of the plane.

Toward the end of the flight, Pia watched out a window. Her excitement surged again as land came into view in the limitless expanse of blue water. Liam woke up as the plane started to descend. The change in altitude didn't seem to affect him at all. The baby dragon joined her in staring out the window.

Pia divided her attention between the scenery outside and studying her son's triangular head with the slender, graceful snout. He was perfectly formed, with every detail that Dragos's dragon form had, only in miniature.

She might have given birth to him, but he was such a mystery to her. His midnight-dark, violet, jewel-like eyes had gone wide with fascination. As a raptor, he probably already had the capacity to see minute details a mile or two away, but she wondered what he really comprehended of the scenery spread out below them. Right now the lines of his body were delicate rather than powerful, but if Dragos was right and Liam did reach his father's size, he would be a juggernaut.

The magic in him burned fiercely. While Liam's Wyr form was a dragon, her blood ran in his veins as much as his father's did. Liam's Power felt cooler to her than the molten corona of Power that boiled out of Dragos. How would that combination manifest in Liam's talents and abilities? All they knew at this point was that he had some of her ability to heal, for he had saved her life before he had ever been born.

She pressed her lips to the top of his head and whispered telepathically, *I love you.*

He closed his eyes and leaned against her cheek with a sigh.

"Come here, little man." Dragos held his hands out to Liam.

Liam's body tightened in protest around Pia's neck. She patted his leg while she bit back a smile. As much as he loved his father, at this stage in his young life he was definitely a mama's boy.

When Dragos spoke again, his dark, rich voice was soothing. "I will give you back to your mother soon enough. For now you must come to me."

While he talked to his son in a low murmur, Liam's body relaxed and his sharp, slender talons slipped out of her T-shirt. He offered no protest when Dragos gathered him up in gentle hands.

Pia stuck fingers in the new holes in her shirt. She muttered, "If this keeps up, I'm going to need a new wardrobe."

She watched Dragos cradle Liam against his chest. As the small, white dragon looked up, Dragos bent his dark head and whispered in Liam's ear for several minutes. Liam rested his head on Dragos's chest as he listened. She couldn't make out specific words, but she felt the effect of Dragos's words in snatches. Reassurance, praise and encouragement radiated from him.

The sight of father and son together never failed to affect her. Dragos was the most lethal and efficient fighter she had ever seen. He had a killing speed along with his immense size, and he had once pulled the crumpled metal of a wrecked car away from her body.

As Dragos held Liam, his hands seemed even more massive on the baby's small body. He had positioned his long, powerful fingers with utmost care at the base of the lacy wings.

The small dragon's body shimmered and changed, and the baby Dragos cradled against his chest had turned human again.

Pia's sigh of relief mingled with a sense of awe. Her father had been human, and she had only learned how to shapeshift into her Wyr form the previous year. Even then she had needed Dragos's help. It had taken Liam less than four months.

Dragos patted Liam's round, diapered bottom. "Well done. Now that you've learned how to shapeshift, you can change back again whenever you need to." He lifted his head and handed the baby back to her.

As she took Liam, she whispered to Dragos, "You win all the good Daddy points."

His eyes glinted with wicked sensuality, and his eyelids lowered to conceal it. Ever the opportunist, he murmured, "And what will that get me?"

"If you play your cards right, it might get you lucky later."

He traced the line of her jaw with his forefinger. "How about if I throw in dinner by the ocean?"

It was a good thing they were both sitting, because that slight caress made her go weak at the knees.

As their gazes connected, all the light banter fell away, leaving something pure and naked, a shock of connection that reverberated through both mind and body. As she stared into his intent gold eyes, the rest of the world fell away. She was caught in a beguilement that would never end, and she would go anywhere with him, do anything for him. She loved him so much, she couldn't breathe.

She fumbled for a good reply. After all, she didn't want him to get too cocky. "Dinner by the ocean might increase your chances a bit."

The sexy, cruel line of his mouth tilted up. He slid one hand to the back of her neck, his fingers pressing lightly. The rasp of calluses against her sensitive skin caused a ripple of sensation to cascade down her body. She licked her lower lip and watched as his gaze fell to track the movement.

Her unsteady lips shaped his name, as she said without sound or air, "Dragos."

Heat flashed out of his tense body, invisible and volcanic. Slowly his fingers curled around the hair at her nape and clenched into a fist. He held her trapped in a possessive, barbaric hold, but everything he did was possessive and barbaric, and she wouldn't change him for the world.

On her lap, Liam burbled companionably and tugged at her shirt. It broke the molten spell burning the air between her and Dragos. She blinked down at the baby.

For a moment she couldn't remember why they were on the plane, or where they were going.

Dragos hadn't loosened his hold on the hair at her nape. He growled very softly, "Tonight."

She managed a shaken nod. She was going to get so lucky tonight.

No, she meant he was.

Sooo lucky.

The plane's angle of descent grew steeper, and near-by land magic began to tickle at her senses. Dragos gently disengaged his fingers from her hair as she turned her attention to the peanut. Liam remained sublimely unaffected by the change in air pressure in the cabin, so she nursed him and changed his diaper while Dragos walked toward the front of the plane to talk with Eva and Hugh.

The last few minutes of their flight raced by, and they touched down at the L. F. Wade International Airport. The airport was small and the runways short, so the plane braked hard and taxied briefly until it rolled to a stop. Within moments the ground crew had the mobile stairway wheeled into place, and they disembarked into hot, bright sunshine.

A Mercedes SUV rental waited for them in the parking lot. They brought their car seat and fitted it to one of the bucket seats. Once Liam had been securely strapped in, Eva drove while Hugh rode shotgun, and Dragos, Liam and Pia rode in the back.

The airport was located on St. David's Island, at the northeast tip of Bermuda. Their house was located on the northwestern tip of the main island, so they drove across the causeway and along S Road. Even though they were on the opposite side of the island, Bermuda was not a large place, and the trip went quickly.

Pia couldn't see everything fast enough and craned her neck to look around at the intense green foliage and palm trees, the colorful variety of buildings and the glimpses of ocean and sandy beaches as they threaded through the streets.

Dragos lounged at her side, watching the passing scenery too. "Did you know that Bermuda has more than five hundred shipwrecks in the shallow reefs that circle the islands, dating from the 1500s?"

Pia turned to stare at him. "Five *hundred*?"

He nodded. "And those are only the ones that have been identified. Some are even popular scuba diving sites."

"The ocean floor must be like a pile of cars in a junkyard. How on earth could you hope to find the *Sebille* in all of that?"

He rubbed his jaw. "Well, if the *Sebille* had wrecked in shallow waters, it would have been discovered a long time ago. If it's out there, it's going to be deep."

She blinked. If it had sunk in deep water, it was no wonder nobody had located the ship yet. "Does that mean you won't be able to find it?"

He shook his head. "There's no way to know. It does mean finding it will be a challenge."

She studied his hard features. The frown that had been a part of his visage for so many months had eased, and he looked relaxed, alert and interested in life. She didn't care about treasure hunting for its own sake, but she was delighted that it had caught Dragos's interest, and the history of the *Sebille* had begun to engage her attention almost in spite of herself.

"How are you going to try to find it?" Most professional shipwreck hunters and maritime archaeologists had highly sophisticated and expensive equipment, and a single expedition could cost hundreds of thousands of dollars.

He lifted one shoulder in a casual shrug. "The first step will be to quarter off the area surrounding the islands. Then I'll search it systematically by flying low over the water. My magic sense is highly developed. In isolated circumstances, I can sense magic from a couple of miles away. The *Sebille* might not have been carrying treasure, but with a voyage that important, it would have carried magic items—at the very least an enchanted sextant for navigating in deep water under heavy cloud cover. And if I sense a spark of magic, I can dive for it."

She tried to imagine diving so deep with all of that water between her and the open air. A shudder tried to take over her limbs. She sternly pushed it down. "Could you dive as deep as the ocean floor?"

He never bothered with machismo swagger, because he didn't need it. He said simply, "Yes."

"What will you do if you don't find anything in the flyovers?"

He shrugged. "Dive anyway until I've thoroughly explored each area. I'll concentrate first on the most likely routes ships sailed from Ireland and expand my radius from there. At that point, if I get serious, I'll look for primary sources in local records. It would help to talk to Tatiana, but she may not be willing to talk about details of the voyage. There might have been secrets on the ship that she would rather leave unfound."

"It sounds like a lot of grueling physical work."

"It is." He sounded pleased at the thought. "It's a lot of flying and swimming, and time spent outdoors in the open air and sun."

She pursed her lips. Maybe while Dragos conducted the physical search, she could do some digging for local sources.

Eva slowed the Mercedes on the narrow paved road, until she pulled to a stop beside a thick, recently trimmed hedge in front of the large, peach-colored villa. A flagstone path cut through an opening in the hedge.

The peanut had fallen asleep in her arms, so Eva opened the car door for her to step out. While Eva and Hugh pulled out the luggage, Dragos joined Pia and they walked up the path.

The house was two stories high and built into a hill. Steps led up to a wraparound porch on the upper level and the main front entrance. As they started up the steps, an attractive human woman in her forties opened the front door. She wore a summer linen suit and ballet flats, her dark hair pulled back in a chignon.

"Welcome, Lord and Lady Cuelebre." She spoke with a crisp British accent and smiled at them. "I'm

Leanne Chambers, the property manager. We're so honored that you've come to visit."

"Hello." Pia returned her smile. "This is a beautiful place. I'm in love with it already."

"Isn't it lovely? This is my favorite of all the rentals I manage." Leanne's dark gaze dropped to Liam, and her smile turned indulgent. "If you like, I can show you straight to the bedroom where I've put the crib."

"Thank you, but if I try to put him down in a strange place, he'll only wake up and fuss."

The other woman inclined her head. "If you'll allow me, I'll give you a quick tour and get out of your way."

She handed two sets of keys to Dragos and led the way through the house, keeping up a light patter of conversation. The house had been built in the late nineteenth century and used as a vacation home ever since. The windows were high and elegant in spacious rooms with hardwood floors, and decorated with simple, comfortable furniture.

Pia could easily picture people in Victorian and Edwardian dress gracing the large parlor room and the living room with the immense fireplace, or playing cards and board games on the veranda. The front lawn was just large enough to contain a croquet set. Pia caught a glimpse of the beach through the trees down the terraced path.

Despite its age, the house had been updated with every modern convenience. An outside shower had been installed so people could rinse off from the beach before stepping inside. The large kitchen had new stainless-steel appliances, and two of the five bathrooms had Jacuzzi tubs. There was only one bedroom that had an *en suite* bathroom, and Pia was pleased to see that it still had the original enameled tiles and claw-foot tub.

Leanne paused in the doorway of the master suite. "I took the liberty of setting the crib in the room beside this one. And because the house is so large, I bought a baby monitor to go with it. Along with filling the grocery order, I've stocked the fridge with four complimentary bottles of white wine, and a fruit-and-candies tray."

Pia smiled at the other woman. "Thank you."

"My pleasure. Is there anything else that you need?"

"I can't think of anything," she replied. "I love this place. Everything is wonderful."

She glanced at Dragos. He had turned on his phone and his head was bent as he studied the screen. Her shoulders drooped. He glanced at her and frowned.

He pocketed his phone and told the manager, "Thank you, that will be all."

"Very good." This time the inclination of Leanne's head was deferential. "I'll see myself out. Enjoy your stay."

Pia moved to look out the window at the sparkling water. The baby snored slightly. He sounded like a squeaky toy. Sleeping soundly had turned him into a dead weight, and her back ached from carrying him around.

Disappointment tried to darken her earlier excitement and pleasure. She had dangled Dragos's favorite hobby in front of him, and they had just arrived in a literal paradise, but he still couldn't keep his phone turned off. When she'd started a relationship with him, she knew she was going to have to share his time and attention, but she never realized how much of a problem that would be, or how much it might grow to bother her at times like this.

Mostly she was fine with it. That wasn't rationalization; she really was. Between the overwhelming demands of his corporate responsibilities and the Wyr demesne, he carried a heavy load, and it suited her just fine to play a supporting role for him. She wasn't as driven as he was, and she absolutely adored the fact that she had the luxury to concentrate on the peanut while he was so small.

Only occasionally, like now, it caused a heavy ache in her chest.

Dragos walked up behind her and put his hands on her shoulders. "What has dimmed that bright smile of yours?"

She tried to think of something positive and supportive to say. "Don't you love it here? This place is gorgeous."

His fingers tightened. He bent over her until his lips touched the thin, sensitive shell of her ear. He whispered, "I turned on my phone to search for a place to go to dinner."

She looked over her shoulder at him. "Really?"

"Really. I've already turned it off again."

The leaden feeling in her chest lightened. At the same time the back of her nose prickled and moisture flooded her eyes. Embarrassed at the sudden surge of emotion, she folded her lips tight and nodded.

His gaze was too keen and filled with understanding. He rubbed her back. "I wouldn't trade this past year away for anything, but it's still been hard on us."

She leaned back against his strong frame, and he wrapped his arms around both her and the baby. "I wouldn't trade it away for anything either."

"Things will get easier, I promise." He rested his cheek on the top of her head. "As soon as all of the sentinels are back at work, let's go upstate and stay for a couple of months."

"Are you sure you can take the time away from the city?" She rested her head against his chest, and he stroked her hair.

"Yes. We'll need to make plans for renovations and building, but we can take things at our own pace and go as slow as we like. If there's an emergency and I have to work, I'll make sure it takes no more than twenty-five hours a week. Kris has been my assistant for so long, he should be able to handle most things. We can take Liam hiking. It will be a real, extended break. How does that sound?"

She had to clear her throat before she could speak again. "I would truly love that."

"I would too." He pressed a kiss to her temple. "Consider it a date."

"Okay." She turned her head toward him, and he nuzzled her.

The baby stirred in her arms, and Liam lifted his sleep-blurred face to look around. His round eyes and soft, open mouth reflected his astonishment at the change in venue. Pia grinned. The last time Liam knew, they had been on the plane.

"Okay, Peanut, time to show you around. Then you get to play with Aunt Eva and Uncle Hugh while I change into fresh clothes, and Mommy and Daddy go out to eat."

"Do you want an upscale restaurant, or a beachside tavern?" Dragos asked. "Because if you want upscale, I have to turn my phone back on again to make a reservation."

She didn't hesitate. "Ooh, beachside, please!"

He grinned. "That's what I thought you'd say, which is why I had already turned it off."

She stood on tiptoe to kiss him. "You know me so well."

He put a hand at the back of her head and held her in place as he returned her kiss lingeringly, setting her body on a slow burn.

"Get ready." His voice was so low it was barely more than a vibration against her lips.

Feeling intoxicated, she nodded as he let her go. She caught the heavy-lidded slant of his glance as he turned away, and she knew he hadn't been talking about their dinner.

Chapter Four

Pia showed Liam the house, along with his room with the crib, his clothes and toys. She knew from past experience that it would be easier to leave him once he saw where he was, and she was right. He didn't fuss when she handed him over to Eva.

Dragos left the master bedroom and bath to her and carried a change of clothes and his toiletry kit into one of the other bathrooms. Pia opened windows, and the sound of the nearby surf washed in.

She hummed as she shaved her legs and washed her hair. After blow-drying her hair, she chose to leave it down and loose. She slipped on a simple, dark blue sheath dress that ended at mid-thigh and flat, silver sandals that complemented her slender feet and legs. She spent the most time on her makeup, enhancing her eyes with a dark, smoky eye shadow and stroking a cranberry-colored lipstick on her lips.

Wearing such rich colors brought an extra sheen out of her thick, light gold hair and made the most of her tan. After she was finished, she stared at herself. Anticipation made her eyes sparkle.

"Look at you," she whispered at the bright, vivid creature in the mirror. "You look happy."

Happy. A year ago she wasn't sure she knew what the word meant.

Sure, in a lot of ways the last year had been hard. Aside from all the other challenges she and Dragos had faced, she still wasn't completely accepted by the Wyr community, and while the peanut had gone a long way to softening everybody's heart, criticism about her unrevealed Wyr form continued to be harsh.

Despite that, her life was pretty damn close to perfect. She had more than she had ever dreamed she could have. She had a husband and mate who adored her with a kind of ferocity that should have been scary but somehow wasn't, and she had the most precious son imaginable. She had friends, good friends, and while they weren't close, even Aryal had abandoned her antagonism toward Pia.

A sudden, superstitious fear chilled her skin. She was too happy.

Happiness this intense couldn't last. Something was bound to happen.

As soon as she had the thought, she clenched her fists and shoved it away. So what if something happened? Something always happened. When it did, she and Dragos would face it as a team, just like they had everything else over the past year. They could handle anything life gave them as long as they were together.

She could handle anything, except for losing either Dragos or Liam.

Angry at herself for letting baseless fear ruin her happy mood, she dragged a brush through her hair one last time, slipped a few things into a small silver purse with a chain-link strap and left the bedroom.

As she walked down the hall, she heard high-pitched baby squeals. In the living room, Dragos tossed Liam into the air and caught him. Liam was giggling so hard his face was almost purple. Nearby, Hugh and Eva lounged on couches, their faces creased with laughter as they watched the pair.

Pia started chuckling too. Liam's paroxysm of delight was simply too infectious to resist. As she walked into the living room, she said, "If it were anybody else doing that…"

Dragos threw Liam into the air again. "I won't let him fall."

"I know you won't."

Dragos had dressed in a black silk polo shirt and cream slacks. His clothes were expensive, simple and lethally effective, as they highlighted the power and grace of his muscled body. While he wasn't much for wearing jewelry, he never took his wedding ring off. He also loved the gold Rolex she had bought him for Christmas, and both it and the braided length of her hair gleamed brightly against his dark copper skin. As he caught the baby one last time and turned to her, she saw that he had shaved as well.

He had made an effort to look nice for her. The knowledge curled into the pit of her stomach and intensified the tug of attraction she always felt for him. She watched him look down her body. When he met her gaze, sultry heat shimmered in his gold eyes.

"I'm hungry," he said, and she knew again he wasn't talking about dinner.

She had to clear her throat. Her voice was huskier than ever as she replied, "Me too."

"Shall we go?"

She nodded and walked over to kiss Liam. Dragos handed the baby to Hugh, and they left.

The heat of the day had begun to ease, and heavy yellow light slanted through the lush greenery as they walked to the Mercedes. She noticed how cleverly the area had been designed to maximize the privacy of the houses, with rows of hedges bordering the narrow road. Dragos opened the passenger door for her, and she climbed into the warm car.

He slid into the driver's seat a moment later. As he turned to her, she asked, "How far away is this beach-side—"

The rest of her question disappeared in a squeak as, eyes glittering, he yanked her to him. He took her mouth in a hard, hot kiss.

Her skin flashed with the heat from his mouth, his hands, and her pulse exploded. Melting against him, she kissed him back as hungrily as he kissed her. His pulse raced to meet hers as he slanted his lips over and over on her, driving deep into her mouth with his tongue.

When he finally lifted his head, they were both shaking. He stroked the disheveled hair away from her face and helped her to ease back into her seat.

"I didn't put a comb in my purse," she said.

"Leave it," he told her, very low.

Laughter shook out of her. "I can't just leave it and walk into public like this. It looks like we've been making out."

One of his black brows lifted as he reached over her to pull her seat belt around her torso and click it into place. "We have."

He was no help. He loved any and all barbaric displays of his claim on her. While he started the car, she ran unsteady fingers through the thick mass until she had the long, tangled strands smoothed out.

The restaurant was on Ireland Island, just a short drive away. After doing her best to tidy her appearance, Pia rolled down her window to let a blast of fresh, ocean-scented air clear her head. The streets were more narrow and winding than she was used to, but Dragos seemed completely comfortable driving on them. He reversed into a cramped parking space that she wasn't sure she would have attempted.

Outside the car, he took her hand as they walked to the beachside restaurant, where music played over loudspeakers. The restaurant was open on the three sides that faced the water, and railings that ran the border all the way around except for the entrance. The fourth side, where the kitchen was located, was solid building. A bar lined the wall between the kitchen and the tables, and a dance floor was set to one side.

The place wasn't fancy. It had wooden tables and concrete floors, but the bar was packed, and so was the dance floor, and the food smelled fabulous. People spilled out onto the beach, drinking and talking together in groups.

Pia studied the scene curiously as she followed Dragos to the bar. There was quite a mix of clientele. Some people were well dressed, but more than not wore jeans or shorts and T-shirts, and many appeared to have just come from the beach. A few looked downright rough, such as the pair of men lounged at the bar.

Space opened up beside them at the bar. Dragos approached.

The two men eyed Dragos speculatively and turned their attention to Pia where their gazes lingered. One of the men was human. He had a wiry build, a beaky face, and long, graying hair pulled back into a ponytail. He wore gold earrings, and he looked at her out of the corner of his eye.

The other man was Light Fae. He was bigger, younger and broader. He was almost as large as Dragos. He, too, had long hair pulled back in a ponytail, only his was blond and curling. He was deeply suntanned, and he wasn't nearly as circumspect as his companion. He stared openly at her breasts and hips.

He thrust out with his hips as he said something to his companion in a language she had never heard before, and the other man laughed.

Their crudity was like a slap in the face. She ignored them, her expression turning stony, but Dragos didn't.

Dragos's immense body turned taut with sudden menace. He turned to face the bigger of the two men, slowly and deliberately, and he took a step forward until he stared down into the man's eyes. He looked hard as granite, his gold eyes flat and deadly.

People around them fell silent, some animal instinct warning them of possible danger.

Pia's breathing constricted. The other man stood his ground, with an arrogant, insolent stance. Although it was hard to believe, clearly the idiot didn't have a clue either who he had ogled, or who he had engaged in a pissing contest. Had he been living under a rock?

She tugged at Dragos's hand.

He ignored her. The tension between the two men ratcheted higher, hovering just on the edge of violence.

Pia wasn't sure what happened next, but the other man's stance changed. He shrugged, said something again in his strange language, and turned away to lean his elbows on the bar where he and his companion muttered together in low voices. Neither man glanced at Pia.

Dragos took a step back. She let go of the breath she had been holding. The crowd relaxed and conversation picked up.

She asked Dragos telepathically, *Was that really necessary?*

He looked at her. *Yes.*

She studied him with a frown. His expression and his body language had relaxed, but his molten gaze was still murderous. *They're just assholes*, she said gently. *Can you let it go, or do you want to go somewhere else for dinner?*

If anything his expression turned angrier at the thought of leaving. *Fuck, no.* He paused and his eyebrows knit together. *Unless you do.*

She smiled up at him. *Thank you for asking, but I'm fine.*

He considered the crowded space, eyes narrowing. *We can find somewhere else to wait for a table.*

I told you, I'm fine. You already backed them down. They're just two dumb jerks, and they're probably drunk to boot. They're not that important.

His expression lightened with approval. She wiggled around him, opposite the other men, and came up to the bar. Dragos came up behind her until his hard body pressed against her back. He slid an arm around her, and she felt totally surrounded, protected and at ease. She couldn't have been safer if she had been locked in a secret vault at Fort Knox. She leaned her head back against his chest to smile at him and finally felt him relax a little. The other two men ignored them as if they were in another room.

The bartender came up to them. Pia ordered a Mai Tai while Dragos ordered scotch, and they put their name on the waiting list for a seat at one of the tables.

She raised her voice to be heard over the music. "So when do you want to start your search?"

"I thought I'd get going first thing tomorrow morning," Dragos said. "Would you and Liam like to come with me for a little while?"

"I'd love to." She sipped her drink. It was delicious. "If you don't mind help, I thought I might check out museums and libraries to see if I can find any mention of the *Sebille*."

He smiled down at her. "I don't mind at all, but don't you want to spend some time on the beach?"

"Sure," she said. "But Bermuda is only, what, twenty miles from end to end?"

"Something like that."

She shrugged, enjoying the excuse to snuggle back against him. "I doubt there will be many places to do research on ancient Elder shipwrecks. I could look around in the morning, and Liam and I can go to the beach afterward."

"Sounds good to me," Dragos said. "We've got a plan for tomorrow."

Something snagged her attention, and she turned her head. The two men beside them had stopped talking. They both leaned against the bar and stared into their drinks, their bodies tense and still.

Her gaze narrowed, and she caught the bigger, younger male glancing at them. All sexual innuendo and crudity had left his expression, leaving him looking cold and hard.

She turned away again quickly. What the hell was his problem? The men might speak a strange language, but they could know English too. Was he listening to her conversation with Dragos, or was he still mad at the unspoken pissing contest he and Dragos had been in? She shook her head. He was going to live a very short life if he didn't either learn to be polite or to let things go.

A waitress came up behind them and took them to their table, which was right by the beach. Pia was so delighted, she put the unpleasantness from the bar firmly behind her and settled in to enjoy the rare treat—a date with Dragos, while he was on vacation.

She ordered a salad with mangos and artichokes. Dragos ordered steak and lobster, and a bottle of Pinot Noir. The server brought the wine right away.

Even before they got their meal, she started plotting.

Due to the inter-demesne functions they had attended over the last year, she had learned how to dance in a formal setting. The experience of waltzing with Dragos was something she would never forget, his power and assurance as he swept her around a ballroom while he looked down at her, unsmiling and severe in his black tie.

She had never seen him dance just for the fun of it, though.

She sighed happily as their server set a beautiful salad in front of her and gave Dragos his meal. When they were alone again, she told him, "I sure love to dance."

Dragos said, "No."

She almost burst out laughing. Instead she raised her eyebrows pointedly. "Don't you love to dance with me?"

Amusement creased the sides of his mouth. He cut into his steak. "What a talent you have for asking loaded questions. You made a political chore very enjoyable. It's important to present a united front and to demonstrate to everyone that we are a team."

"You don't have a romantic bone in your body, do you?" She grinned and thought about teasing him some more, but he had been so responsive about taking a vacation, she decided to take pity on him and relent.

"Never mind. I'll just have to enjoy those waltzes enough for the both of us."

They talked more about plans for moving upstate, and the decision became more real with conversation. While they had made the decision because it was best for Liam, by the end of the meal Pia started to look forward to the change.

After all, young parents move to the 'burbs all the time, for all kinds of reasons. To get away from crime, to get away from the noise and crowdedness of the city. To raise their children in greater peace and safety, and to give them greater freedom to roam.

Raising a magic baby dragon wasn't so *very* different.

She thought of the long, lone flights Dragos took periodically to relieve the stresses of city life.

She said, "This is going to be good for all of us."

"I think it will too. I'm starting to look forward to it." He took the last bite of his lobster and set his fork down. "Do you want dessert or coffee?"

While Dragos didn't have much of a sweet tooth, she did, and he often chose to have a cheese plate and port to keep her company. She shrugged. "I could take it or leave it."

"Then come on." He stood and held out a hand.

Obligingly, she slid out of her seat and slipped her fingers into his grasp. "We haven't paid yet. What are we doing?"

He slanted a black eyebrow at her. "We're dancing."

She went into delighted shock. He led her onto the dance floor.

Chapter Five

No, Dragos didn't have a romantic bone in his body, but Pia made it easy for him. Whenever he did something for her, she lit up with pleasure. Her midnight-violet eyes sparkled, and joy glowed from her skin. Canny businessman that he was, he invested in her happiness and reaped the returns in bright laughter, soft smiles, gentle touches and impulsive hugs.

His world turned grim when she was unhappy, and his thoughts became aggressive and bladelike. He grew intolerant and quick to slash out. He did not trust a world that had the audacity to hurt his mate. Her happiness filled him with contentment.

What was a little dancing compared to that?

They reached the crowded floor. Without the discipline and structure of a waltz, he wasn't sure what he should do. He stood, hands on his hips, as he studied the movements of the other dancers. Some of them looked like they had been tasered and were shuddering just before they collapsed.

That, he would not do. Could not.

Pia touched his biceps. When he looked down at her, her face brimmed with… Okay, that was more than just joy. That was laughter, too.

"Just move." She put her hands on his hips. "Don't overthink it. Listen to the music, do what you want and be natural."

Do what you want. Those instructions were easy enough to follow.

He tugged her close, and she came readily to him, wrapping her arms around his waist. However, she did more than just hug him. She rubbed her slender, curvy body against his rhythmically, twisting and swaying in time to the music, and Dragos's opinion about dancing underwent a drastic change.

He stared at the sinfully gorgeous woman in his arms. She slid along his body with such sensuous grace she set his skin smoldering.

"You know, Dragos," she said with an upward glance and a twinkle, "when two people are dancing, it usually requires both of them to do something."

At her words, his attention snapped to the music. The song was a popular one, bright, quirky and with a strong, tribal beat. He caught the rhythm of it and began to move, and it wiped the laughter off Pia's face.

Holding her gaze, he set his hands on her hips and guided her to move with him. They swayed and undulated together. After a year of living as mates, he was so attuned to her, he could anticipate what she did. Ever the aggressor, he bent forward, and she bowed back. She draped one arm around his neck, her gaze never leaving his.

The music changed, and the next song was darker, smokier. It wormed its way into his blood, and the rest of the world fell away. Their movements together, hip to hip and thigh to thigh, were as necessary and as elemental as sex. The connection between them was always present, but now it grew bright and taut like a bridge of fire.

Sometimes he grew afraid that he burned too hot, that the roar he felt in his blood for her would overwhelm or frighten her, but she never turned from him or backed away. Instead she met his fire with a fierce passion of her own, her cooler, moonlit energy burnishing under the force of his attention until she shone.

She straightened and tugged at the same time, and he bent his head. She whispered in his ear, "If you don't take me out of here, I'm going to come right on the dance floor."

Each word caressed his ear. Her lips were trembling.

It doused him in a sheet of flame. He took her arm and led her off the floor. Everything happened from a distance, on the other side of the urgency that pounded in his body.

To the exit. Someone came and bleated at him. Their server. He dug in his pocket and shoved cash at her without counting it. The server stepped back, beaming.

Away from the beach, toward the car.

The sun had set while they ate their dinner. White light from halogen street lamps threw pools of light along the streets and the beach, heightening the darkness beyond. Pia almost stumbled, but his tight hold wouldn't let her. She looked etched, the contours of her face marked with tension. His sharp predator's eye caught the subtle shift of her slender throat muscles as she swallowed. Her scent was feminine and musky at once, and he listened to the tiny friction of her silk dress against her skin.

They reached the Mercedes. As he looked at it he thought of the myriad, complex movements it would take to drive the machine. How mundane. How human. The dragon rebelled at the thought.

He wrapped them in a cloak of invisibility and picked her up. A muffled noise came out of her. It sounded stark and needy. She hooked her arm around his neck as he strode to the edge of the parking lot. A waist-high stone wall separated the asphalt from the sand. He leaped it and ran down the beach, faster and faster until the wind whipped through their hair.

Within moments they left behind the bright lights of the dockyard and the incessant chatter of humanity. The ocean murmured against the sand in a rhythm far older than any music. Lights dotted the dark shoreline, and a slice of moon curved in the dark blue, starred night, but the place he found was deep with shadows.

He walked into the deepest of the shadows, where the line of trees and bushes met the beach. Only then did he set her on her feet. Now her whole body trembled. He could hear her heart racing.

He did that. He caused her body to shake and cry out. He set her heart racing, made her laugh, created her happiness. He reached past the bone and sinew of her body and touched the invisible, mysterious core of her, the place that defined her.

That place. *That* invisible, mysterious place was his home.

He lived for it. He would die for it.

It did not define him. He was too old and too wicked. But if he were ever to believe in a place called Eden, paradise or heaven, that invisible place would be it. It had nothing to do with forgiveness. It was more necessary to him than redemption.

She could break him. Him. In their year together, the surprise had still not left him. He had lived through cataclysms. He had survived the undying enmity of Elves and the shifting of continents, but she held his old, jaded heart in her two slender hands.

"Here?" she whispered.

"Here," he told her. "Now."

He pushed her against the trunk of a tree and went to his knees in front of her. Sliding his hands up the taut, graceful line of her thighs, he made a startling discovery.

She wore no panties underneath that short—*very short*—thin dress.

Her audacity shocked a growl out of him. He cupped her round, silken-smooth ass and buried his face greedily in the soft, private hair at the juncture of her thighs.

She gasped, shaking all over, and leaned back against the tree while she hooked one of her fabulous legs over his shoulder, opening herself for his exploration. He licked and suckled at the velvety, succulent flesh of her sex. She was slick and inviting, and she tasted like arousal.

The sensation shot down his spine. His already hard cock stiffened further until he felt thick and swollen.

Gods, he loved to fuck her, with his tongue, his fingers, and his penis—anything he could use to get inside her most private place, and to feel how she responded to him. He inserted his forefinger into her gently, feeling how her inner muscles gripped him.

Her body vibrated with tension as her pleasure escalated. She cupped the back of his head with trembling fingers as he found the stiff little nubbin of her clitoris and licked. He inserted a second finger. She arched her back as she accommodated him, and her moisture coated his hand.

"You need this," he growled. "Say it."

"Yes." She stroked her fingers through his hair.

"You need me."

He knew what he sounded like. He sounded arrogant and demanding, and slightly ridiculous, but she didn't seem to mind.

"Yes!" she cried out.

He used the back of his knuckle to press her clitoris to his mouth, rubbed his teeth gently, gently across the delicate, delicious flesh and felt the shock waves shudder through her body. She shoved a hand against her mouth to muffle a cry.

His own need was growing urgent, and his pants felt too tight. Too civilized. He unzipped and yanked them open to let his engorged penis spill out, never once letting up from working on her.

The incantation he wove on her was his greatest enchantment. Each stroke, lick and thrust was a line that made a verse, each verse necessary and building on each other to create the final spell. She showed him the way the spell should be cast with every gasp and flex of her muscles, every tiny betrayal revealing the intensity of her pleasure.

Her tension escalated until it broke apart. She bucked against his hold and forgot to muffle her cry when she climaxed. The tiny shock waves rippled through her muscles. He felt it through his fingers as he stroked her deep inside, at the site of her second pleasure center, while he never stopped licking.

She was so hot, so tight. He was dying to sheathe himself in her, but he held himself under rigid control while he sucked hard and drove in with his fingers at the same time—and she convulsed again, sobbing.

That's it, he murmured in her head. *There you are. Give it to me again.*

She shook her head jerkily. "I can't—Those blew my mind. I can't—I can't stand up any longer."

Yes, you can, he told her. *I'm going to take you right up against that tree trunk. Right after you come for me one more time.*

"Good God, Dragos!" She clenched her fingers in his short hair.

He fucked her with his fingers while he never let up on the pressure with his tongue. The heat coming off of her body was unbelievably erotic. She made a strangled, mewling noise at the back of her throat, and the sound went straight to his cock. In that moment, he was absolutely sure he was going to die if he didn't get inside of her just as quickly as he could.

Swearing, she bent over and draped across his shoulder, and her inner muscles clenched on his fingers as she came one more time. He wrapped an arm around her neck while he cupped her until the orgasm eased.

He was breathing like he had raced a marathon, his own need turning his muscles rigid. As he loosened his hold on her, she slid into his lap. He yanked her torso closer, and she wrapped her legs around his waist as she reached between them.

The sensation of her slender fingers closing over his erection was delicious, agonizing. His head fell back, and he sucked in air through clenched teeth as she stroked him.

"Come here," she whispered.

He widened his thighs, spreading her legs as she raised herself up and rubbed the tip of his erection against her soft, drenched entrance. Slowly she sank down on him. It didn't matter how many times they had made love over the last year. The sensation of piercing into her body was indescribable. Every time it was like the first time, like new. A guttural groan broke out of his mouth.

He couldn't get inside deeply enough. He gripped her and thrust with his hips. The friction of sliding into her tight, wet sheath made him crazy, crazy. Her moonlit hair was tousled and shadowed her face. Watching his expression with wise, loving eyes, she flexed on him as she undulated her torso. She knew exactly what to do, and it sent him over the edge.

Gripping her tighter, he pumped once, twice, three times hard and fast. The climax ran through the muscles of his body, hitting him like a steamroller, and he felt himself beginning to pulse inside of her. The pleasure was so violent it was almost excruciating.

"Fuck me," he gasped.

"Any time you want," she whispered. She stroked his face and gave him a siren's smile. "Any time, anywhere."

The aftershocks were still hitting him, pleasure slowly spiraling him down to sanity once again. He pulled her closer, one hand at the back of her neck and the other arm wrapped around her waist. "Always."

She laid her head on his shoulder and pressed her lips to his neck. "Forever."

The mating frenzy that had gripped them last year was never too far away, and for a moment he wavered on the edge. He could take her over and over, passion blazing through the night like a comet. They had done it before, and no doubt would do it again.

For the moment, instead, peace stole over him gradually, until the dragon let go and eased back, and he could think more humanlike thoughts.

"I think I might be able to drive now," he said.

She snickered. "Are you sure?"

He smiled into her neck. "Pretty sure. When we reached the car earlier, all I could think of was: Key. Ignition. Stick shift. Wheel. And then: No."

She laughed harder. "When you picked me up, all I could think of was: Yay!"

"Sometimes the single-syllable conversations are the most important ones." He kissed her and fell into the private, voluptuous world of exploring her soft, sensual mouth.

She murmured wordlessly, the sound filled with contentment, and kissed him back as she stroked her fingers through his hair. They both sighed with regret when his softening penis slipped out of her.

She said against his mouth, "I think I have sand burn on my knees."

He shifted immediately to help her stand. "I'm sorry."

"No, don't be sorry. If it had been really irritating, I would have said something."

Together they brushed the sand off her legs. "We should be heading back anyway."

"As long as you cloak us again on the way to the car. I'm not fit to be seen in public." She tried to straighten her dress while he zipped up his pants.

He paused to look at her with a private, possessive smile. While he liked displays of his claim on her—disheveled hair, lipstick gone, or even the slight evidence of marks on her neck—no, at the moment, she was not fit to be seen in public. The thin material of her dress was crumpled, and they both smelled like sex, and that was too private to be shared.

"Of course," he said. "Are you ready?"

She nodded. This time he took her hand and they walked back, enjoying the night and the breeze that blew off the ocean. When they got back within sight of the bright lights and busy dockyard, Dragos wrapped the concealment cloak around them again.

Pia said, "I am horribly in love with you, you know."

He put his arm around her shoulders. "As I am with you. Horribly."

Her sigh made him smile. It was such a happy sound. He pulled her closer as they strolled toward the car.

Chapter Six

Early the next morning, Pia dressed in Capri cargo pants, a lemon-yellow tank top and her slender silver sandals. Dragos dressed simply as well, in jeans and a gray T-shirt that stretched across the breadth of his chest and biceps.

After a quick, cheerful breakfast, Pia slipped Liam into his baby carrier and strapped him to her torso. She and Dragos walked the path to the beach, where Dragos changed into his dragon form.

Liam crowed with excitement and craned his neck to look at Dragos. Pia turned so he could study his father, and he flailed his arms.

"This is one excited baby." She jerked her head back with a laugh as one of his chubby fists clipped her on the chin.

The dragon bent his immense head and nosed Liam, who shrieked happily and pounded the dragon's snout. Pia laughed harder as she imagined what they might look like to a total stranger. If she had witnessed such a bizarre sight without knowing any of them, she would have been absolutely terrified for the baby and the woman holding him.

The dragon's huge gold eyes danced. He said to Pia, "Are you ready?"

"You bet."

Dragos scooped Pia into one forepaw with extreme care and twisted to set her on his back. With the familiarity of long practice, she scooted up to the natural hollow where the base of the dragon's neck met his shoulders. As soon as she settled into place, she patted his dusky bronze hide. "All set."

Her heart leaped as he crouched and launched over the water in a breathtaking surge of power. It never got old. Dragos's lunges into the air used to scare her, since for flights like this, she rode him without a strap or harness of any kind, but her confidence and trust had grown over time. Even in his dragon form, he was blindingly fast. Once, she had started to slide from her perch, and he had twisted in midair to snatch her up in one paw before she fell.

However, this flight didn't go as planned. When they went airborne, Liam gave another happy shriek—and shapeshifted.

Astonished, Pia stared down at him. Normally when he rode in the baby carrier, he was strapped snugly against the front of her body, but his dragon form was much longer and leaner than his human baby form, and now the carrier hung loose around his sleek body.

He began to crawl onto her shoulders. She threw her arms tightly around him. He wriggled to get away from her, his head turned and jewel-bright eyes fixed on Dragos's huge, flapping wings.

"We've got a problem," she called out.

Immediately Dragos stopped his ascent, spread his wings wide and coasted. He tried to look around, but he couldn't twist far enough to see what happened at the base of his neck. "What's wrong?"

"Liam changed again—he's trying to get away from me. I don't know if I can hold on to him!"

She grabbed Liam by one foreleg and wrapped her fingers around the base of one wing as he freed it from the carrier. Liam flapped his wing and smacked her in the face. Pain flared as he hit her in the nose. Her eyes watered.

Dragos said, "Let him go."

Pia blinked the tears from her eyes and looked around, her thoughts racing. They were already a couple of hundred yards out from shore. If she let Liam go and he tried to fly but couldn't, Dragos would to have to lunge to catch him. If he did, she didn't know if she could hold her seat, or if Dragos could catch them both if they fell.

But it quickly became clear that they might both fall anyway. Liam's strength in his dragon form was sobering. He wasn't even fighting with her. She could tell he was excited, not distressed, but he was so determined she could barely hold on to him.

Thank God they were flying over the water. She thought of hitting the surface at the speed they were going. It might hurt, but at this height, it wouldn't kill her. It would help if she controlled her fall and hit the surface in a dive.

"Okay," she said. "Ready?"

"Yes."

She let go of Liam. He pulled free from the carrier, balanced on her shoulders and launched into the air. Heart in her throat, she watched as he flapped his wings enthusiastically and…

Plummeted in an ungainly spiral.

"Watch out, he's falling!" she shouted.

Fear clutched her. Strong though he might be, he was still a baby. She might survive if she hit the water, but the fall could kill him.

Quick as a cat, Dragos twisted and snatched him out of the air. "Got him."

"Jesus wept." She hunched over Dragos's neck, leaning on one hand. "That sight aged me twenty years."

Dragos wheeled and flew back to shore. When he landed, he knelt so Pia could slide to the ground. She managed to do so without falling, which was a major feat since her legs were shaking so badly. She walked around to face him.

He held the small, white dragon in one cupped paw. As she joined them, he turned his paw upward and opened his talons. Liam leaped and flapped his wings madly, and fell in a sprawl on the beach. He rolled to his feet and crouched to spring into the air again.

Dragos put a paw on him. "*NO.*"

Liam froze.

Dragos picked him up, held him between two talons and regarded him. The small, white dragon hung meekly limp in his grasp.

Dragos offered Liam to Pia, who gathered him in her arms. Suddenly sitting down seemed like a good idea. She plopped on the sand, crossed her legs and cuddled the baby. Liam rested his head on her shoulder, his expression thoughtful.

Dragos's Wyr form disappeared as he shapeshifted. Glancing quickly along the deserted beach, he walked over to kneel beside her and they both contemplated the graceful white form of their son.

Uncertainty chewed at Pia. She angled her head up to Dragos. "Are we terrible parents? I mean, who takes their baby up in the air like that?"

"We're excellent parents. What we did was natural and normal. Avian Wyr take their babies in the air all the time."

He sounded so sensible. She tried to calm down. "My heart almost stopped when I watched him fall."

"He was never in any danger." Dragos looked deeply into her eyes. "Neither were you. If you had fallen with him, I would have caught you too. This wasn't any different than me tossing him in the air and catching him in the living room. You just got scared. That's all."

She put her cheek down on top of the white dragon's head. "Avian Wyr really do that?"

"Yes, they do." He rubbed her back, his touch slow and soothing. "In fact, falling is part of learning to fly. Clearly Liam and I will need to go out and do some practicing. You're welcome to come up with us if you want."

"No, thanks. I think I'll stay on the ground for those lessons." She shook her head and rubbed the back of her neck. "He's going to be able to fly before he's a year old. We need to get a toddler leash and hire avian nannies."

"We will. It's all right."

Gradually her heart stopped its headlong pounding as she listened to him. She considered Dragos's expression. He was entirely calm. In fact, the only thing he evidenced was mild concern for her.

She came to the humbling realization that she was the only one who had panicked. "You weren't bothered in the slightest by what happened, were you?"

He managed to produce a vaguely apologetic expression. "I'm afraid not."

Blowing out a breath, she glanced down at Liam. He lifted his head and smiled at her. Good God, look at those teeth. Baby though he was, with those teeth and razor-sharp talons, Liam could do some serious damage to someone if he had a mind to, yet the only thing he had done so far is damage her clothes.

He was already being careful.

She stroked his head. "You're such a good boy. I'm so proud of you."

He leaned into her hand and sighed.

"I guess our morning flight is cancelled," Dragos said.

Liam's head popped up. His expression turned stricken.

Pia steeled her heart against the sight. The primary reason they had come to Bermuda in the first place was so that Dragos would get some time for rest and recreation.

"That's all right." She smiled at Dragos. "Why don't you start your search? We don't need to come with you. I'll start on the research." She turned her attention to Liam. "If you want to come with me, you need to change back into your human form. Otherwise you have to stay here with Uncle Hugh."

Liam's gaze slid sideways to Dragos.

Pia told the baby firmly, "No, you're not going with your dad. You can go flying with him soon, but not this morning."

Thunderclouds gathered in his violet eyes. He growled.

A thoroughly annoyed baby dragon was quite a sight. Her face compressed, and she bit both of her lips. She would *not* laugh.

Dragos tapped Liam's snout. "Stop that. Don't growl at your mother."

The peanut blinked and jumped. Giving her an apologetic look, he changed, and she held her innocuous, human-looking baby in her arms.

She cuddled him close. "That's better."

Dragos kissed the top of Liam's head then kissed her on the mouth. "I'm going to take off."

"Have fun."

"You too." He paused. "Don't do anything you don't want to do. If it gets boring, stop."

"Don't worry about me. We'll have fun and be fine." She shooed him. "Go. Be free."

He smiled and changed, stepped a few paces away from them and leaped. Dragos had taught her some time ago how to see beyond the cloaking spell. She watched him soar, the dragon's huge wingspan conquering the air. No matter how long she lived, she would never get tired of that sight.

Back at the house, she found Eva and Hugh drinking coffee and reading newspapers that Hugh had picked up earlier from the local grocery store. They both looked up as she entered the kitchen. Eva asked, "Did you have a nice flight?"

"Well, we had an eventful one." Pia told them wryly what had happened. Eva groaned but Hugh just laughed. Pia regarded him with a sour expression. "Do gargoyles really take their babies on flights?"

"Every chance we get." Hugh grinned. "In some clans, the parents toss 'em off a cliff."

She shuddered. "And there for a while I thought we were the worst parents ever."

"Not so," he replied. "Hitting the ground in our gargoyle form doesn't hurt us. If a baby gargoyle gets that far, he'll just bounce."

She thought of Hugh's hard, stonelike façade when he was in his Wyr form. Still, she said doubtfully, "If you say so."

Eva slapped her hands on her thighs. "Enough about that. Ready to go exploring?"

Pia bounced on the balls of her feet. "Yep. Let's go."

They headed out the door. Eva drove again while Hugh took shotgun, and Pia rode in the back beside Liam in his car seat.

Eva glanced in the rear view mirror. "I poked around online while you guys were out to dinner last night. There's an Elder museum located in an old lighthouse on the west coast of Somerset Island. You wanna start there?"

"Absolutely." Pia smiled with satisfaction.

The drive took about twenty minutes, and a good section of the route followed the coast. After a brilliant rose-and-gold dawn, the late morning remained perfect, sunny and cloudless. Light sparkled off the intense blue ocean. Both motor and sailboats dotted the water.

The Elder museum was located in the Beacon Hill lighthouse, which sat on the edge of land that jutted into the water. The white-and-red lighthouse towered against a backdrop of blue sky and water. Slowing, Eva turned the Mercedes down a narrow lane.

Pia looked around with interest as Eva pulled into a small, half-full parking lot. A few picnic benches were scattered across a wide lawn, and a Dark Fae family sat at one of the tables eating ice cream. Across the lawn, two trolls sat side by side, their faces tilted up to the sun. They looked like boulders that someone had carved faces on. At the far side of the building, a tall man with a ponytail leaned against the corner.

Pia's eyes narrowed. The man stood in the shade, and it was impossible to make out his features from the parking lot. His hair was dark, not blond. Could it be the human male from the bar?

If so, it was a hell of a coincidence for him to be hanging out here, after their run-in last night. She thought of how the two males had gone silent and tense while she and Dragos had talked. What exactly had they discussed?

They couldn't have mentioned the lighthouse. She had only found out about it this morning when Eva told her. But Bermuda was a small place. "Eva, you didn't find anywhere else for us to do research, did you?"

"Nope, unless you want to check out the Bermuda Maritime Museum. That'll be focused more on human history, so I think you might want to call first before making a trip over there."

Pia stepped out of the Mercedes, shading her eyes. Moving quicker than his nonchalant attitude would have suggested, Hugh joined her. The man pushed away from the building in the other direction and disappeared.

Hugh asked, "What's up?"

"Come with me." She told Eva, "Watch the baby."

She strode across the parking lot with Hugh at her side. Hugh said, "If you saw something you think is dangerous, you'd better tell me."

"I don't know what I saw." Unsettled, Pia's gaze swept over the people at the picnic tables again. "Just a man leaning against the side of the building, here at the corner."

They reached the spot where they could see the far side of the building. A narrow path led alongside the building and down the hill. Pia rubbed the back of her head and tried to decide how paranoid she was, while Hugh stood watching her patiently.

She started on the path but was brought up short by Hugh's hand on her arm. "You wanna see what's down this path, okay, but I'll go first."

Impatiently, she gestured for him to go ahead of her then followed close behind, glancing up once at the lighthouse that towered high overhead. They reached the farthest corner of the building that faced the ocean, and walked to the edge of a sharp drop where they surveyed the scene.

The path cut down a short, rocky bluff to a pier where a motorboat carried a single male occupant with a dark ponytail. The boat headed out to sea.

Hugh angled his head at Pia. His usual sleepy expression had vanished, and he looked alert and interested. "What now?"

She blew out a breath. "Now we go back to the car, and I'll tell you and Eva about what happened last night."

They retraced their steps along the path. Pia paused where the man had been standing as they pulled up. She caught a faint whiff of cigarette smoke, along with a male scent.

Hugh inhaled deeply. "I'll remember his scent."

"So will I."

He narrowed his eyes. "Does this guy have anything to do with what happened last night?"

She shook her head. "I can't tell. We were in a bar with cooking food and a lot of people packed up against each other, and I didn't get close to him. Come on, let's get back to Eva and Liam."

The Mercedes idled, engine running, in the parking space. When they approached, she heard a mechanical click as Eva unlocked the doors. She and Hugh climbed into the air conditioned vehicle.

Pia told them about the men at the bar. She frowned. "I'm pretty sure that Dragos and I talked about starting the search for the *Sebille*, but I can't remember what exactly we said to each other."

"And you feel like they didn't recognize you or Dragos." Eva didn't frame it as a question.

Pia shrugged impatiently. "I don't even know that the man today had anything to do with last night. I just saw a guy with a ponytail and remembered the men at the bar. Maybe I'm being paranoid."

"Paranoid is a lot better than stupid, sugar." Eva drummed her fingers thoughtfully against the steering wheel. "And we're gonna keep on being paranoid. Hugh, go scout out the museum before we head inside."

"Be right back." Hugh slid out of the SUV and ambled toward the building.

He returned in a few minutes. Eva rolled down her window as he approached the driver's side. "The guy's scent is definitely inside, but the museum's all clear."

Pia unbuckled the straps on Liam's car seat and lifted him out. "Let's take a look around."

Chapter Seven

Inside, the museum took the entire ground floor. Aged wooden floors, colorful posters and display cases lured the eye. One section of shelves, lined with books, was roped off and someone had taped a computer-printed CLOSED sign to the rope.

Normally Pia would have been interested in looking around, but at the moment, she was too focused. Flanked by a watchful Eva, she walked through the museum and looked for a curator or attendant while Hugh strolled through the displays.

After some searching, she finally located a dwarf sitting at a desk in a back office, and she paused. The dwarf was dressed in jeans and a T-shirt with the museum's logo, and had a beard, but that was no indication of gender.

The office also carried a distinct male scent, with a whiff of cigarette smoke. Pia told Eva telepathically, *The man from outside has been in here very recently, within the last couple of hours.*

The plot thickens. Eva looked happy, but then Eva loved a challenge, and she usually looked happy when something got complicated or went wrong. *I didn't even know we had a plot on this trip.*

Pia said aloud, "Excuse me, could you answer a few questions for us?"

The dwarf jumped, knocked a sheaf of papers and exclaimed in a clearly feminine voice, "Gods! You startled me."

"I'm sorry." Pia started forward. "Let me help."

"No, no, never mind." The dwarf waved Pia away without looking at her. She slid out of her chair and onto her knees to gather up the papers. "Whatever you want, you'll have to make it quick. I'm very busy today."

Pia said, "I just wanted to know if the museum might have any historical records or information about an old Light Fae ship named the *Sebille* from the early fifteenth century."

"No," the dwarf replied, her voice flat. She still hadn't raised her head. She stacked the papers together. "I'm afraid I can't help you. We don't have anything."

Something about other woman's demeanor seemed off, but her instincts had gone into hyper drive, so for the moment she reserved judgment. "Can you recommend anywhere else in Bermuda where we might research the *Sebille*?"

"None of the other island museums have anything." The dwarf's tone had turned short to the point of rudeness. She rose to her feet and slapped the papers on the desk.

Pia exchanged a glance with Eva and shook her head. That wasn't just her imagination. Something definitely wasn't right. "You sound very sure of that."

"I am very sure," said the dwarf. "This is the only museum of Elder history in Bermuda."

"But you've heard of the *Sebille*," Eva pressed. "You know what ship we're talking about."

"Of course I've heard of it," the dwarf replied irritably. "Every couple of years some fool comes through, itching to learn everything they can about the *Sebille*, and they want to scour the records here for any mention of the ship. I'm going to tell you the same thing I tell all the others." She finally looked at Pia, and her small, dark eyes were anxious. "Don't waste your time. Go enjoy your vacation, and play with that cute baby. Stop searching for the ship."

Pia's gaze narrowed. She said softly, "Talking about it seems to bother you for some reason. Are you all right? You're not afraid of someone, are you? Because if you are, we can help you."

The dwarf drew in a quick breath and lowered her voice. "Wait a minute, I know who you are. Look, there are some men who have been looking for that ship for a very long time—since before I came to Bermuda and took over the museum. I'm not sure how many men, and I don't know where they live. I don't want to know. All I know is they spend time at the dockyards a lot, and they frequent bars, and their leader…he's not a nice man."

Eva and Pia exchanged another glance. Pia asked, "The leader wouldn't happen to be a big Light Fae male, would he? Long hair pulled back in a ponytail?"

The dwarf rubbed her chin nervously with the back of one hand and nodded.

"And one of his men was in here earlier to talk to you." Pia didn't ask it as a question.

The dwarf nodded again. "Years ago, I used to have a few records that mentioned the *Sebille*. There was nothing substantial, mind you, just mainly some stuff that has been retold so much it's turned into legend. A massive storm and strange lights in the sky, that sort of thing."

"Strange lights." Eva's eyes narrowed. "What kind of strange lights?"

The dwarf snorted. "It was probably just lightning in the clouds. A few people claimed that they sighted the ship from the north shore, and then it disappeared."

Pia felt a thrill of excitement. "So it was sighted here."

The dwarf threw up her hands. "Apparently so, and people have been looking for it ever since. Like I said, every once in a while they show up here, just like you did. They want to dig for clues. But something always happens to them. Their boats disappear, or they have an accident. Somebody always ends up getting hurt. So I got rid of the records. I burned them. And I tell people I don't have anything, and to stop looking." She sniffed. "Sometimes they don't listen, but I still try."

"What about the man who was here earlier?" Pia asked. "He didn't threaten you, did he?"

The dwarf shook her head. "No, they don't bother with me. I wouldn't hunt for that damn wreck if my life depended on it. He wanted to know if anybody had been in today to ask about the *Sebille*. He must have been on the lookout for you."

Eva said gently, "If they come looking for us, they're not going to like what they find."

Dragos flew away from the islands in a bright flood of sunshine. After a short while, he left the shallow reefs behind and soared over deep water. He concentrated on flying thoroughly over a section before going on to the next, searching in a circular pattern around the islands. He made a complete pass all the way around, then moved outward in greater concentric circles.

Most people would have found it tedious work, but he didn't. He reveled in the solitude and freedom as he soaked up the sun's brilliant warmth. The air smelled briny and clean over the ocean. It felt good to stretch out his wings and work his body, and good to truly let go of crowded city life. He put away considerations of politics, stocks and profit margins, and let the dragon take over his thoughts.

The vast, tangled mass of land magic that made up the Bermuda Triangle lay to the west. He considered it without much curiosity. A few of the crossover passageways came in quite close to land, but passageways in the ocean were easy to avoid. All he had to do was fly high enough overhead.

He grew hungry, dove for fish and ate while he flew.

He covered more than a hundred miles in an hour. Within a few hours, he grew convinced that the *Sebille* had not foundered anywhere near the edge of the shallow reefs bordering the islands, and he headed farther out in a wider circle.

Dragos? Pia said.

Like every other Wyr, her telepathic range was quite limited, but Dragos's telepathic range was much larger than the average Wyr's, and he heard her quite clearly.

Yes? he replied. *Are you having a good morning?*

We're certainly having an interesting morning. How about you?

I'm having a great time, he told her. *It's beautiful out here.*

Her mental voice warmed. *I'm so glad.*

He banked and wheeled toward the east to start another circuit. *Did you find out anything at the museum?*

Yes, we actually found out quite a bit more than we expected. Her voice sounded a little odd.

He cocked his head. *Tell me.*

Apparently the Sebille *was sighted off the north shore in a big storm, and then it disappeared again. At least that's what the curator told us was in old records before she destroyed them.*

His interest quickened. If the *Sebille* was sighted off the north shore, he could try narrowing his search area down by doing some calculations of the currents. He left the area he had been searching, whirled in a big circle and began to follow the ocean's current north of the island. *Why did she destroy them?*

Because there's a group of men who have been searching for the wreck for a long time, and they don't take kindly to competition, Pia told him. *They've been scaring off anybody who goes looking for it. The curator said the treasure hunters' boats sink or disappear, and somebody always got hurt, so she finally destroyed the records. She said their leader is a big Light Fae male, and he's not a nice man.*

Dragos did not bother to snort. He was not a nice man either.

He said thoughtfully, *A big Light Fae male?*

Yes, and when we got to the museum, there was a man hanging around the building. He left as soon as we arrived. She paused. *He had been inside the museum before we got there, and he wanted to know if anybody had been in asking about the* Sebille.

Was it one of the men from the bar? His thoughts turned dark and murderous.

I don't know, but it might have been. Who else would have known that someone would be showing up at the museum this morning? You and I talked about it last night.

I remember, he said. *What are you doing now?*

We're going back to the house, she told him. *I want to feed the peanut and put him down for a nap.*

Okay, let me know when you get there. I'll be back soon.

Don't hurry back for our sake, okay? We're not going to let some pissant local thug ruin our vacation. Eva and Hugh are on alert. We're fine.

All right, he told her. *I'll still be back soon.*

In a matter of minutes he had followed the current past the last of the islands and out to deep sea. Then he continued straight over deeper water.

Almost five miles out from the island, he felt a faint tickle of magic from below. He wheeled around the area.

A moment later, Pia spoke again. *We're back at the house, and Eva and Hugh have thoroughly searched the whole property. Everything is peaceful. Nothing is out of place, and there aren't any strange scents.*

Okay, good, he replied. *I followed the current that wraps around the north shore, and I'm about five miles out from land. I found something. I'm going to dive.*

That's fantastic! Good luck!

He folded his wings and plunged headfirst into the waves. This far out, the water was quite cold. He found it pleasantly bracing. He burrowed down, past where the sunlight penetrated, into frigid darkness.

The pressure increased, and he knew he had dived deeper than most creatures could have survived without protection gear. Soon he had passed the limit of most manned submersibles.

Except for submarine canyons, most of Earth's ocean floors were no deeper than six thousand meters. Still, that was almost 3.75 miles. Aside from the strange marina life that was bred to survive on the ocean floor, very few creatures could survive reaching such depths. The mysterious, powerful kraken could, and so could Dragos, but only for brief periods of time.

To conserve his energy, he swam in complete darkness, following the spark of magic blind, until he sensed that he had gotten close. Then he threw a simple spell and brought light to the dense water.

The light spell illuminated the area roughly twenty-five feet around him in a strange bluish green. The pressure was so intense, he felt like he was digging his way through the water, not swimming. He pushed farther downward, until the light touched on the greenish ocean floor. His lungs had started to burn. He wouldn't be able to stay for much longer.

He kicked his way along the ocean floor, still searching mostly by his magic sense. A few crustaceans scuttled away from the light.

When the wreck came into view, it did so all at once. It sprawled along the ocean floor with the supporting planks of the hull exposed like the rib cage of a dead animal.

By now, Dragos's lungs were on fire, but he was unable to pull away. This close, he could tell there were multiple sparks of magic coming from inside the hull. He kicked along the length of the wreck, searching as quickly as he could for some kind of identification. Going by the size and shape of the ruins, it had been a caravel ship, which placed it in the right historical era. The wreck was as long as he was if he included his tail, roughly forty feet in length.

He drew closer to the port side. The wreck had deteriorated a lot over the centuries, but enough remained that he could see a significant, jagged break toward the rear of the ship. Quite a bit of the hull had sheared away long ago, leaving only the ribs curving up from the base of the ship's spine.

He plunged both front paws into the sediment along the floor, searching for pieces of the hull. As he found fragments of wood, he turned them over and discarded them until he unearthed one piece, roughly a yard and a half in length, that had letters inlaid in silver at one end.

ille.

Triumph surged, but he didn't have time to savor it. He needed air too badly and couldn't stay underwater any longer. Black spots danced in front of his eyes. Carrying the fragment of wood, he kicked to the surface to suck in huge draughts of air. As soon as he caught his breath, he launched out of the water and flew back toward land.

In order to have enough room to change, he had to land on the beach just outside the house. Still gripping the hull fragment, he strode up the terraced path.

Pia had been keeping an eye out for him, because he had barely stepped out of the tree line and onto the lawn when the door opened and she hurried out. Her eyes shone with excitement. "What is it? What did you find?"

He held up the piece of wood, letters facing outward, for her to see. "I think I found the *Sebille*."

Chapter Eight

"Already? That's amazing." She touched the blackened letters on the wood wonderingly.

He grinned. "I would have found it eventually, but I got lucky. I used what you gave me and followed the current off the north shore. The wreck is quite a ways out and it's deep. It's no wonder nobody has found it before now. There's only a few submersibles in the world that can dive down that far."

Pia glanced at him with an inward smile. He always had a vital, powerful presence, but now his dark bronze skin looked burnished, and his gold eyes shone with radiance. "Come inside and tell me all about it. Liam's gone down for a nap. Eva and Hugh barbequed steaks for lunch, and they set aside plenty for you."

His expression flared with interest. He propped the plank beside the back door and followed her inside. The interior was much cooler than outside. They had closed up the house and turned on the air condition. While he washed up, Pia piled the steaks on a plate for him and set it on the dining room table in the large, sunlit kitchen.

He thanked her as he sat at the table and began to eat. Pia eased into the seat across from him, and Eva and

Hugh came to join them while Dragos told him about his flight and the search in between large bites of the juicy meat.

"By the time I found it, I was getting tired and needed air, so I wasn't able to stay down for very long." He sprinkled salt on the steak. "I didn't have a chance to examine the wreck too closely, but I did notice there was a jagged break toward the back third of the ship, between where the main mast would have been and the rear mast. It would have been a hell of a storm to cause that kind of damage. Poor bastards never had a chance."

"So there is at least one magic item with the wreck?" Pia asked.

"Yes." He polished off the last bite with a satisfied sigh. "In fact there are several. I want to go back down, maybe first thing tomorrow morning, and see what I can bring up."

Pia nodded. "I wish I could come with you."

Pushing away his plate, he crossed his arms on the table and smiled at her. "You could, at least in a boat. You would have to wait on the surface, but if we took a boat out, I could make a couple of dives to bring things back up."

She clapped her hands. "Let's rent one!"

He grinned. "You bet."

Eva spoke up. "I looked through the brochures the rental agency left. You can rent a boat from them. I'll give them a call."

"Great." Pia looked at Dragos. "So that's tomorrow morning. What do you want to do this afternoon?"

"You relax, enjoy the sun." Dragos pushed away from the table and stood. His face turned sharp as a blade. "I'm going to go on the hunt for a big Light Fae male who is not a nice man."

Pia stood too, quickly. That dangerous face was so sexy it made her knees weak. Sometimes she still wasn't quite sure of her reactions to Dragos. "I'm coming with you."

His inky-black eyebrows drew together in a frown. "I don't think that's a good idea."

"Well, I do." She put her hands on her hips. "You know what's going to happen if we find him. He's going to be an asshole, and, Dragos, you can't kill him just because he's an asshole. You're not Lord of these islands."

He regarded her with a dark expression. "Fine. Come on."

Pia looked at Eva. "We'll be back later."

The other woman's face was full of suppressed amusement. "Have fun."

Dragos went out the back door to get the plank of wood, which he set on the floor of the backseat of the Mercedes. They took off.

That afternoon Pia developed a healthy respect for how many bars, restaurants, grocery and marina supply stores, and fishing shops could be found in the Bermuda islands. Dragos was single-minded and didn't tire, and she was determined to keep up with him.

They scored a hit with their perseverance in Hamilton Harbor a couple of hours later. After Dragos parked, they walked along the rows of shops and bars at the edge of the marina.

Almost immediately, Dragos's nostrils flared. "He's here. Hold on a minute."

Dragos had literally been in the Light Fae male's face last night, so he had to have gotten a good fix on the other male's scent. Thank God. Pia was hot, tired and thirsty. She just didn't have a hunter's drive or instinct. If it had been up to her, she would have quit searching an hour ago.

She stood waiting while he strode back to the SUV. When he returned, he gripped the plank in one hand. Then he led the way unerringly to a bar located at the end of the lane, pushed open the door and strode in.

Bracing herself for whatever came next, Pia followed.

Inside, the décor was sturdy rather than elegant. Wide windows faced the water. They had been propped open in the heat of the day. Wooden tables dotted the floor, and tall stools lined the bar against the interior wall. Loud music played, the place was crowded, and it smelled of alcohol and fried food.

Pia spotted the Light Fae male right away, leaning against the bar. This time he appeared to be alone.

Despite the noisy, crowded atmosphere, Dragos's fiery presence drew attention. People fell silent, and the clink of cutlery against dishes ceased.

At the bar, the Light Fae male turned. His eyes narrowed as he caught sight of Dragos and Pia. He straightened, and his smile was more of a sneer.

"Get out," Dragos said. The dragon was in his voice.

Except for the Light Fae male, all the customers rushed for the door. Pia barely had time to move aside. Within seconds the place was empty except for, Dragos, Pia, the Light Fae male, and the bartender and wait staff who moved to one side of the room as they watched nervously.

The scene should have been ridiculous, but somehow it wasn't. Dragos tossed the plank onto the floor in front of the other man, and the Light Fae male's sneering smile vanished.

"I located the *Sebille*." Dragos strolled toward the other man. "And I'm going to bring up everything I can from it."

The Light Fae male's gaze flared as he stared at the plank at his feet. When he looked up again at Dragos, his gaze had turned flat and ugly. He said in a strongly accented voice, "That wreck, and everything on it, is mine. You made a big mistake, and not a healthy one for either you or your pretty companion."

Pia heaved a sigh. He did not just say that, did he? To Dragos, of all people.

Dragos blurred. He took hold of the Light Fae male in both hands, lifted him in the air and twisted at the waist to slam him into a table so hard the table collapsed, with him on it. Dragos followed him down, kneeling to hold the other man pinned by the throat.

"Aaaand, that's assault and battery," Pia muttered.

Did officials in another country have the legal authority to throw the head of an Elder demesne in jail? She didn't know the answer to that. Not that it necessarily mattered, since the question was purely hypothetical. If it came to that, the authorities couldn't trap him long enough to put him in jail, and anyway, Dragos would demolish any building with jail cells in it. The whole thing would become a legal snarl that would clog up the Elder tribunal for months and years. No wonder Dragos's lawyers were so rich. He was a litigator's wet dream.

She pinched the bridge of her nose to stave off a growing headache. She noticed one of the waitstaff was on the phone, no doubt calling the local police.

The Light Fae male struggled, but he could gain no purchase against the iron hand that gripped him. "Your mistakes are getting worse, my friend," he hissed. "There are many more of us than there are of you."

"You dare to threaten me?" Dragos hauled the Light Fae male close to his hard, angry face. "My wife says that I can't kill you for being an asshole. She has a much kinder heart than I do. If you or any of your men come anywhere near us, I will take you apart. Slowly."

The Light Fae male's face purpled. He clawed at Dragos's hand and spat out a long string of words in the strange language Pia had noticed last night. She didn't have to understand what he said to know he wasn't apologizing.

Pia tried smiling at the waitstaff. They stared at her, frozen. She said, "We'll pay for the damages, of course, and for everybody's meal."

Dragos threw the Light Fae male one-handed across the room. He slammed into the wall and slumped to the floor. Then Dragos stood. He was so quick, so inhumanly graceful for his massive size, that just the simple movement of rising to his feet made the skin at the back of Pia's neck prickle.

It would set a very bad precedent if he had any clue how he affected her when he behaved so badly, so she tried to play it cool. "You've had your fun. Are you done now?"

Eyes still glowing with fury, he stretched his neck and nodded. He bent to pick up the plank and said to the bartender, "Send the bill to Cuelebre Enterprises."

The bartender nodded.

The Light Fae male lifted his head. His expression underwent a drastic transformation. "*Draco.*"

Finally. Now that the other male had realized who Dragos was, maybe he would grow some sanity and leave them the hell alone.

Dragos reached Pia, his face like a thundercloud. She held the door open for him. Neither one of them said a word until they had walked back to the SUV. He unlocked the doors with the key fob and threw the plank into the backseat again while Pia climbed in the front.

Sirens sounded in the distance. They grew closer rapidly. For a moment neither Pia nor Dragos moved.

She didn't even try to hold back on the sarcasm. "I think it went well, don't you?"

Dragos angled his head and just looked at her. Then he started the engine and drove them back to the house.

When they stepped indoors, Pia tried to shake off the tension that had bunched the muscles between her shoulders. Liam had woken up from his nap and was playing on the floor. As he caught sight of them, he squealed in excitement and crawled toward them.

Dragos scooped him up and sat on one of the couches. Smiling at the baby's happiness, she joined them.

It took the authorities forty-five minutes to find them. When the knock came at the door, Pia took Liam and grinned at Dragos. "We're going to go play somewhere else for a while."

His mouth twitched. Enough time had gone by to allow for his temper to lighten. "Have fun."

Eva followed Pia and Liam outside, carrying wineglasses and a blanket to spread out on for the baby. They walked down to the beach.

Pia settled on one corner of the blanket. Seagulls hovered over silver-capped waves. The early-evening sun on the water was simply spectacular. She took a deep, satisfying breath of fresh air. "You know, a year ago, I would have stayed in the living room to talk to the police with him, and I would have been all twisted up and anxious about it. Then I realized this stuff doesn't bother Dragos at all. And I mean, not in the slightest. So why should I get wound up if he doesn't?"

"You shouldn't." Eva kicked one foot over the other and stretched out.

Liam pointed at the seagulls, crowed and flapped his arms. Pia and Eva laughed at his round eyes and excited expression.

Twenty minutes later Dragos strolled onto the beach. He told Eva, "Why don't you and Hugh take the evening off?"

"You sure?" Eva climbed to her feet. "We haven't really done anything since we got here."

Dragos looked at Pia, who nodded. "I'm sure," he replied. "Just stay close, and stay aware. Let us know if you notice anything that seems off."

"Will do." Eva grinned. "Have a good evening."

"Thanks, you too," Pia said. Dragos stretched out on the blanket beside her. She handed him her glass of wine while Liam crawled energetically over to climb on his legs. "What did the police have to say?"

"Not much." He handed the glass back to her, stripped off his T-shirt and stretched out with his arms behind his head. "The Light Fae's name is Rageon Merrous, and he's been on their radar for some time. He started showing up on the islands around forty years ago. He's been linked to the disappearance of a few people and implicated in accidents involving others, but they haven't actually caught him in a crime, nor have they been able to bring charges against him for anything specific. He was gone from the bar by the time they got there. They're going to send a police car to patrol this neighborhood while we're here."

The sight of his bare chest never failed to bring down the level of her concentration. His physique was simply tremendous. A sprinkle of black hair arrowed down the heavy, powerful muscles in his chest. She laid a hand on the ridged muscles of his warm abdomen and looked out to sea so that she could gain some coherency of mind again. He placed one hand over hers and laced their fingers together.

She asked, "Why does he think the *Sebille* is his?"

He moved under her hand in a shrug. "Who knows? Maybe he's a family member of one of the ship's crew. Maybe he feels he's entitled to it because he's been looking for the wreck for so long. Treasure hunters are an obsessive lot, and they can get pretty crazy, especially if they've sunk any kind of capital into a serious search."

"If he's a family member, does he have a point? I mean, would he have a claim on anything in the wreck?"

"There's a difference in maritime law regarding salvage versus treasure hunting. Salvage involves recovering property where owners have the right to compensation or return of their property. Treasure hunting is a separate matter, because usually there's no owner to make a claim on the property." He shrugged again. "That gets more tangled in Elder law, since so many of us are so long-lived. In this case, though, it's fairly simple. The one with any potentially legitimate claim is Tatiana as the sponsor of the original expedition. The bottom line is, Merrous doesn't have a leg to stand on."

She contemplated that for a few moments. "What about Tatiana?"

"If she's interested in whatever is on that wreck, she can file a petition with the Elder tribunal." He yawned. "But it's just as likely she won't care enough to pay the legal costs."

She had to smile to herself. Of course he knew so much about treasure rights in maritime law. "So that's it."

"Pretty much." He closed his eyes. "Unless you let me kill him."

"Oh, no," she said strongly, twisting at the waist to scowl at him. "You cannot put that on me. You know as well as I do, you can't kill somebody just because they're an asshole. We've heard some hearsay and a lot of suspicion, but we don't know if Merrous has actually done anything wrong. If he becomes a real problem, then one way or another we'll take care of him. Until then, all of this is just male posturing and hot air."

His smile was lazy and relaxed. "Fair enough."

Liam had managed to climb on top of Dragos's legs. Now he crawled up his father's torso, his small face determined. As Liam kneed Dragos in the crotch, Dragos jackknifed onto his side, laughing, and they dropped the subject for the evening.

After a while Pia went up to the house to collect snacks and another bottle of wine for dinner, and they stayed out on the beach to watch the sunset. She nursed the baby, who fell asleep on her. She, in turn, curled against Dragos's chest, while he put his arms around her. When she tilted her head back to smile at him, he covered her mouth with his and kissed her with a slow, leisurely thoroughness that never failed to heat her blood.

Happy, she thought. *I'm too happy.*

She banished that traitorous thought firmly and eventually fell asleep.

She woke sometime later to movement. Dragos had wrapped her and the baby in the blanket and carried them up the path to the house. She yawned and mumbled, "Stuff on the beach."

"We'll get it in the morning," he said quietly.

He carried them through the shadowed, empty house and laid them gently on the bed. Then he gathered up Liam's small, sleeping form to carry him to his crib in the other bedroom. Pia yawned again so widely her jaw popped and pushed off the bed to go to the bathroom, wash up and brush her teeth. On the way back to bed, she peeled off her clothes and let them drop to the floor. Those could be picked up in the morning too.

A few minutes later, Dragos joined her. She rolled toward him as he slid under the covers. He was naked too, and she sighed as she came up against his long, muscled body. The comfort of nestling skin to skin with him was indescribable. She needed it as much as she needed air, or food. She rubbed her face against the warm skin of his chest while he ran his hands down the curves of her body and caressed her breasts. He let out a quiet hiss when she stroked his large, hard erection and the tight, full sac underneath.

She gave herself over to languid instinct and slid down the sheets while he rolled onto his back and stroked her hair. By now they knew how this dance would go, but instead of familiarity breeding boredom, it fueled the excitement.

She knew what would happen when she put her mouth on him. She knew what he tasted like, and she craved it. She craved him. It was an incomparably sweet ache that leavened every part of her day. She lived her life in a state of constant questioning.

Where will he be next? When will I see him again? In the living room? In the kitchen? Will we have time to shower together in the morning?

How can I bear to be apart from him for an entire day?

Sometimes they didn't manage it, and they came together in a heated rush at lunchtime. Then they created a fire that burned so beautifully.

That was how she felt then, as she opened her mouth and took him in. She sucked on the broad head of his penis, swirling her tongue around the small slit at the tip. He swore, a low, rapid stream of unintelligible words, while his body turned rigid.

It hurts, it hurts, she wanted to tell him. But she had lost the capacity for telepathy. A tear slipped down her cheek from the ache of it. She opened her throat and took him all in. He pumped into her mouth, hips flexing. She could not get close enough, could not take him in deeply enough.

When he grasped her head in both hands and pulled her away, she made a needy sound and tried to pull him back to her. He refused, hauled her bodily up the bed and came between her knees. Then she understood what he wanted, and she welcomed him greedily.

"I can't ever get enough of you," he whispered against her mouth as he positioned the tip of his cock at her opening.

"Me neither. Hurry." She gripped the back of his neck.

He pierced her, drew back and pierced her again, and that was the thing she needed, as they came together in the most intimate dance of all. She lifted her hips to meet his thrusts, flexing inside in the way she knew would bring him the most pleasure.

He gasped, shook his head and quickened the rhythm. Then he leaned on one arm and slid a hand between them. She was so ready, she climaxed as soon as he touched her. A high, thin whine came out of her, and she shook all over as the exquisite ripples conquered her body.

He thrust harder and quicker, once, twice, and then he arched his back as his own climax came. She held her breath so that she could feel everything as the hard, thick length of him pulsed inside of her.

There. There. Such sweet, beautiful fire.

Chapter Nine

In the morning, Liam enjoyed a long, lovely cuddle in bed with Mommy and Daddy. Then he grew excited because Mommy and Daddy started getting ready to go somewhere. Often that meant he got to go somewhere too, and he liked exploring this new, sunny place.

They said things to each other like, "Do you have our sat phone?" And: "They're bringing the boat to the pier on the beach."

He would have preferred to fly, but a boat sounded promising. In fact everything sounded promising, but then Mommy started saying things like, "You get to have fun with Aunt Eva and Uncle Hugh this morning."

He tried to ignore her, because sometimes she changed her mind, but soon it became clear that Mommy and Daddy were leaving, while he had to stay. When they kissed him and left, he turned exceedingly cranky. But it was hard to stay mad for long, because Aunt Eva and Uncle Hugh *were* fun.

He was determined to stay awake until Mommy and Daddy got home, but despite his best efforts his eyes grew heavy. Hugh carried him to the bedroom and tucked him in the crib. He watched with sleepy interest while Hugh checked the room. Hugh tugged at the handle of the closed window as he looked outside, then he pulled the curtains shut and left.

Liam yawned, fell asleep and woke some time later.

Fresh air sounded nice—fresh air and wind, and flying.

Daddy had said *NO*, but that had happened quite a while ago. Surely by now *NO* had turned into a *YES*.

In fact, he was all but certain of it.

He was a very helpful peanut. Mommy and Daddy were busy on a boat, so he would take himself out to practice flying.

He shapeshifted, crawled out of the crib and climbed the curtains to the closed window. He tugged at the handle.

Over his head, the latch clicked and the window slid open.

Pleased, he climbed onto the sill. Each day his balance got better. He looked out happily at the hot, sunny day. Aunt Eva walked by underneath. He watched her curiously, then she went around the corner of the house, and he forgot about her.

A flicker of movement caught his eye, and his head snapped around. A bright green lizard wandered down the road on the other side of the hedge.

Hm, hungry now. That lizard looked tasty.

He spread his wings and leaped into the air. Flapping as hard as he could, he half-flew, half-coasted to the other side of the hedge and landed in a tumble on the gravel shoulder beside the road. It startled the lizard into running alongside a row of parked cars.

Instinct kicked in. Liam rolled onto his feet and ran after the lizard. When he flapped his wings again, he rose into the air and flew several yards. Excited, he ran some more, jumped and flew several more yards. They ran down the road like that until, in a final lunge, he managed to grab the lizard's tail.

The lizard struggled as he dragged it toward him. To his immense surprise, it pulled away from its tail and ran away again. Confused, he looked down at the tail he still held in one forepaw. Then he ate it. Um, delicious.

Now he really wanted the rest of that lizard. Where had it gone? He walked, looking around and peering under cars, but the lizard was nowhere in sight.

A car door opened a few feet away, and a man stepped out to walk toward him. He was a human with a long, dark ponytail, and he stank like cigarette smoke.

"Well, well, well," said the man in a friendly voice. He shrugged out of a jean jacket and held it in front of him as he drew closer. "What have we got here? Why, you look just like a baby dragon."

Liam sat back on his haunches and smiled at him.

The man recoiled. "*Christos!*"

The man threw the jacket at Liam. Darkness descended as it settled over his head. He struggled to get free of the heavy material, but the man scooped him up in his arms and held on tight. Then they were bouncing—the man was running.

Liam growled. He didn't like this game.

"Shut up." The man no longer sounded friendly.

A car door opened. The world shifted and swayed, and the man held him on his lap. The car door shut again. They were in a car. It accelerated.

"What have you got wrapped in your jacket?" It was another man's voice.

"It looks like a small dragon," said his captor. "I think it's his kid."

✧   ✧   ✧

Pia and Dragos decided to take the boat out for a couple of hours, so they didn't bother to pack any food, just plenty of drinking water. While Pia watched the changing landscape, Dragos piloted the boat skillfully between all the other traffic on the water. It didn't take them long to leave land behind altogether.

The boat was a much slower method of transportation than Dragos in flight, but he knew where he was going so he could take them directly to the spot.

When they reached the area, Dragos killed the motor, and Pia turned in a circle, marveling in the sight of water all around her without any sight of land. He told her, "The anchor won't do any good out here. You're going to drift, but don't worry about it. You won't go far."

"Okay." She grinned at him. "Go on, don't worry about me."

He nodded. "See you soon."

They had brought one of their emptied suitcases along. He tossed it into the water, leaped overboard and swam far enough away so that he could shapeshift without capsizing the boat. Then the dragon appeared and gave her a huge wink as it hooked the handle of the suitcase in one talon. With a great splash, he dove.

How long would it take him to find the wreck? She had no way to know, so she relaxed in one of the seats and watched the waves.

The endless vista of sparkling ocean was remarkably hypnotic, and the sight had lulled her half asleep when she heard a great splash. She jerked upright and swiveled around to see the dragon swimming toward her with the suitcase clutched in one paw.

As he drew near, he shimmered into a change and became the man. The boat rocked as he grabbed the short ladder toward the rear on the port side. He held on, gasping. She hovered nearby. "Can I help?"

He shook his head. "It's really heavy. Watch out."

She stepped back, and he climbed up the ladder with the suitcase dangling from one hand. He heaved it into the boat, and it landed with a spray of cold water and a solid thud. Then he knelt beside the case, unzipped it and flipped the lid back.

Gold winked at them. There were also blackened objects that Pia couldn't identify, possibly tarnished silver items. There were coins, and a small chest, and something that looked mechanical and felt magical.

"Wow. Just, wow." She pointed to it. "Is that a sextant?"

He nodded, still breathing hard. He fingered a coin as he said, "This stuff was half buried and in leather bags that deteriorated when I tried to pick them up. There's probably enough to fill two more suitcases down below. Tatiana wanted to find a new land badly, and she was willing to pay for it."

"What do you want to do?" Pia asked. "You can dump out what's in the suitcase, go back down and collect the rest of it now, if you want."

He shook his head. "It's not going anywhere. We can go back, and I'll buy some containers to haul it all in."

"Well, if you're sure—" she began. The sat phone rang. She reached for it and clicked it on. "Hello?"

"It's Eva." Eva didn't sound like herself, her voice harsh and ragged. "Liam's gone."

"What?" The words were perfectly audible, but they came out of nowhere, and they made no sense. Pia shook her head. "I'm sorry, what did you say?"

"Liam is missing," Eva said, enunciating carefully. "He's *missing*, Pia. We put him down for a nap, and now he's gone. The house was locked tight. Hugh stayed inside, and I walked the yard outside, but the window in his bedroom is wide open and he is fucking *gone*—"

"Oh my God." Pia's world bottomed out. The sat phone fell from her nerveless fingers.

Dragos didn't need to ask what had been said; he had already heard it. His bronze skin turned ashen, his eyes stark.

Eva was still talking. The words sounded far away and small coming from the phone. As Pia reached for the phone, Dragos crouched and sprang into the air, leaping so hard the boat rocked wildly and knocked her back against the side. He shapeshifted in midair and snatched her up in one claw. He tore through the sky, his huge body straining as they arrowed back to the islands.

Pia went numb. She couldn't feel her feet, or her lips. "The phone!"

Dragos said tensely, "I'm talking to her. They found Liam's scent outside and followed it. It disappeared down the road. The man from the bar—not Merrous, the other one—his scent was at the spot where Liam's stopped."

"Oh God, oh God." This reality was outrageous, nightmarish beyond belief. She screamed, "Are you telling me those bastards have my baby?"

The dragon growled and flew harder.

A hollow, roaring silence filled her mind. Time stopped and started in fitful spurts.

They reached the island and slammed to earth. Dragos shapeshifted again, but only partially. He was gigantic, monstrous, his face and muscles contorted, his hands long with lethally sharp talons.

Occasionally Wyr went into a partial shapeshift in times of extremity. At other times, some could even shapeshift small changes like bringing out their talons, but Pia had only seen Dragos caught in the monstrous half-shift once, when they had mated last year. In spite of her shock over Liam and how much she loved him, she almost recoiled from the sight.

But he was her mate, and she had never needed a monster more than she did right now. He snatched her hand, and they raced up the path.

✧   ✧   ✧

As they neared the house, the dragon let go of Pia's hand and lunged ahead, his long legs eating up the distance. He slammed through the door so hard it tore off its hinges, and he bounded up the stairs to his son's bedroom. It looked serene, with nothing displaced. He scented everything carefully. Nobody had been in Liam's room except for him, Pia, Eva and Hugh.

The window was wide open, and Liam's scent was on the sill. He looked outside. Pia had run around the house and was talking to Eva and Hugh. The body-guards' bodies were tense, their eyes heartsick.

He leaped down the stairs and tore out of the house to join the others. Eva pointed to a spot in the road. "Liam's scent starts here."

He reached the spot and looked back at the house. He could see Liam's open window. He raced to follow Liam's scent to the place where it stopped, and he caught the human's scent and followed that to where it stopped.

After that there was nowhere else to go. Feeling a rare sense of impotence and terror, he stood with his taloned fists clenched. They had gotten into a car. By now they could be on a boat.

And while Liam could understand a great deal, his verbal skills had not caught up with his comprehension. Dragos might be able to reach him telepathically, but he couldn't reply.

Dragos could telepathize with someone else, though.

Merrous, said the dragon in a calm, quiet voice.

After a moment, Merrous gave a telepathic chuckle. *Well, this is uncomfortable and unexpected, but surprisingly useful. I was going to send you a burner phone, but this works even better. I have something of yours.*

He said, *Prove it.*

What do you want, a picture or a body part? Merrous laughed.

He had quite a sense of humor for a dead man. The dragon flexed his talons, and nearby, Eva and Hugh blanched. His voice grew gentler. *Do you want the* Sebille? *Because you will never have it without me.*

Merrous's laughter vanished. He said venomously, *Yes, I want the* Sebille, *and I want everything that went down with it. I presume you want this rug rat back. We'll do an exchange.*

When? he asked. *Where?*

I'll let you know when I work something out. Now, stop talking to me, or someone is liable to get hurt.

Rage filled his body like burning acid. Dragos looked at Pia and the other two. They had been watching his face closely. "I just talked to Merrous. He says he wants an exchange, and he'll get back to me once he decides when and where." He paused as a sliver of rational thought sliced through the lava running through his mind. "He sounds too confident."

Pia grabbed his arm, her fingers biting into his skin. "What do you mean?"

He shook his head as he thought it through. Instinct settled into certainty. "He knows we're Wyr, so he has to have some idea of our tracking skills. Right now he thinks he can't be tracked, which means he's on a boat."

Pia's voice shook. "He can't have gone too far, but there are a lot of boats out there."

"There's only one boat that will have their scents, so we cloak ourselves and go hunting." He looked at Hugh. "I need you to fly out and check every vessel headed away from shore. If he's thought this through at all, he will be expecting us to do that. I think he's acting like someone fishing or on vacation. He'll either be moored somewhere or he's moving very slowly. He'll be hiding in plain sight. We've got to move fast."

"Right." Hugh shapeshifted and launched.

"I need a gun," Pia said. Eva shoved hers into Pia's hands then drew a backup gun from an ankle holster.

"Let's go." Dragos shapeshifted, and the two women climbed on his back. Then he launched into the air too.

Chapter Ten

Liam was starting to feel sorry for himself.

It had been a strange and interesting day, and he had learned a lot. He had flown! Well, a little bit, anyway. And lizard's tails were delicious. A man had given him his jacket, and had taken him on a car ride. Now he was on a boat. The man took his jacket back only to shove him quickly into a cage and slam and lock the door.

Liam sat and waited for something else to happen. Maybe Mommy and Daddy were on this boat, and they would come get him.

Nothing happened. Mommy and Daddy didn't come, and the cage smelled like dog. The boat's engine ran for a while then stopped, and they rocked with the waves.

Nobody came to play with him or bring him food. He had woken up hungry, and he only grew hungrier. And more thirsty.

After a while he looked around the cage. No blanket. No food. No bunny.

He heaved a big sigh and pushed at the door of the cage. When the lock sprang open, he walked out.

He explored the room. It was filled with interesting things like rope, metal tanks, boxes and tarps. Still nothing to eat or drink. He left the room and padded down a short hall. Voices sounded from another room. One of them was the man with the jacket. Liam didn't know the other one.

Smoke wafted out of the room. His nose wrinkled. He didn't want to visit with them anymore. He wanted Mommy.

There were stairs at the end of the hall. He climbed up, found himself on a deck and looked around. There were two more strange men in a cabin. He didn't want to visit with them either, and the shore looked awfully small. He eyed it doubtfully. It was much too far for him to fly. He started to realize just how far away Mommy might be.

His eyes filled. That was the saddest thing he had ever thought in his whole life.

Then another thought occurred to him. He had flown the farthest when he had been the highest—from the window of his room. Maybe if he climbed up to the top of the boat he could fly to shore.

He hopped and flapped and climbed. The boat had a motor, but it also had sails. He swarmed up the sail to the very top of the mast, and there he perched. He looked from the boat to land, and back to the boat.

Now he was very high in the air, but the shore still seemed awfully far away—too far away for him to fly. The boat rocked, and he flapped his wings to keep his balance on his small perch. He did not want to climb down and visit the men again. He couldn't fly away.

He wasn't sure because he'd only heard the word once before, but he thought he might be in a quandary.

✧   ✧   ✧

While Hugh flew farther out to sea, Dragos swung to the nearest pier and dove low over each boat. Pia could feel the dragon's body straining to move as fast as he could while still covering every boat thoroughly before he moved on to the next pier or the next boat that moved at a leisurely pace over the water. They caught wafts of scents from each one—people, alcohol, cooking food, and occasionally cigarette smoke, which was particularly odorous. Dragos always banked and swung around to double-check each boat that smelled like smoke.

She clenched her fists. This search was an excruciating gamble, but the alternative was to do nothing and wait, and that was unthinkable.

Eva sat behind her. "Pia, I don't know what to say," she said, her voice low and shaken. "I am so desperately sorry this happened. We did everything we usually do. Hugh swore he checked the room when he put Liam down for a nap, even though nobody had been in there since you got him up this morning. I swear to you, the house was locked up tight."

Locked.

Pia's head came up. "Oh, shit."

"What?" Dragos asked sharply.

"I was just wondering yesterday what talents or attributes he might have gotten from me." She pressed her fists against her temples. "No lock can hold him. He did it himself. He climbed out the window, and he must have flown to the road."

Dragos turned so sharply, both women rocked in their seats. In a burst of power, he drove away from the boats they had been circling and hammered through the air. "I see him."

Pia's heart leaped. Maybe there was a way out of this nightmare after all. "You *see* him—where?"

"He's perched at the top of a mast, half a mile ahead." A strange mélange of emotions threaded Dragos's voice.

She shaded her eyes, squinting against the bright light. His predator's eyes were much sharper than hers. She couldn't see him.

"A quarter mile away now," said Dragos. "Dead ahead."

Then she caught sight of him. He was a small, white figure and from this distance looked very much like a large seagull, flapping his wings every once in a while as the boat rocked. She didn't know whether to laugh or cry. "Oh, thank you, God."

Thank you, thank you.

"Quiet now," Dragos ordered. "We don't have him yet."

He slowed as he approached the boat, spread his wings and coasted. As they passed overhead like a mammoth ghost, he reached out with one forepaw and scooped Liam up with unerring accuracy. Pia caught a whiff of cigarette smoke as they passed.

Dragos put on a burst of speed. "Got him!"

The unbearable tension broke. She buried her face in her hands and sobbed.

"Hold on," Dragos murmured gently. She wasn't sure if he was talking to her, or to Liam. "We're almost there."

He flew straight to shore and landed on a nearby promontory. Pia fell off his back before he came to a full stop, and she landed jarringly on her hands and knees. She ignored the pain and shoved to her feet, turning to face Dragos as he opened up his paw.

Liam exploded out in a flurry of white wings. He arrowed straight toward her and slammed into her chest. She sprawled on the ground with the breath knocked out of her. She didn't care. She didn't need to breathe. She clenched him to her.

Hard, strong arms lifted her up, and Dragos held them both tight against his chest, his head bent over them. Liam lifted his snout and licked his father's face with frantic enthusiasm.

The moment was too painful to be a happy one, too full of the terror of the last few hours, and she embraced it with her whole heart. She stroked Liam's head, soothing him, and he voluntarily shapeshifted back into his human form and clutched her shirt with both hands.

After a few moments, Dragos lifted his head. His haggard face was damp. "I have a promise to keep."

"Go," she said. "Do it."

He turned a murderous expression toward the boat, stood and walked away. Eva joined her as he shapeshifted into the dragon again and took off. The women watched the sun gleam off his powerful form.

Eva gripped her shoulder. "He isn't cloaking himself. He wants them to see him coming."

They were too far away to hear any shouts or cries, but the sound of gunshots cracked across the water. Even though she knew that bullets couldn't penetrate the dragon's thick, tough hide, Pia twitched at every one.

Dragos reached the boat, slammed into the mast, took hold of it in both forepaws and snapped it in two. Small, faraway figures leaped into the water as he tore the boat to shreds with a savagery that took Pia's breath. As the pieces sank under foaming waves, he rose to hover in the air and turn his attention to the men who swam away.

"Nobody threatens my family and lives." The dragon's deep voice rolled over the waves like thunder. "Nobody."

He plummeted down.

Pia turned her attention to Liam's wide-eyed, round little face. "Don't look, my love," she said gently. She put a hand over his eyes and turned away from the sight.

Liam was clingy when they got back to the house. Pia didn't blame him. She felt clingy too. He whined and indicated he was hungry. Dragos pulled a roast chicken from the fridge and set it on the kitchen floor so he could eat. She and Dragos sat on the floor beside him, while Eva and Hugh stood in the doorway and watched.

He gorged until his belly was visibly distended. Then he climbed into Pia's lap. She pored over every inch of his slender, white body to make sure he hadn't been injured in any way, and she pressed careful fingers against his rib cage and legs. He didn't evidence any sign of pain or discomfort. Instead he stretched under her touch, sighing with pleasure, and fell deeply, instantly asleep.

"The young are incredibly resilient," Dragos murmured. He put a hand lightly on top of Liam's head.

"For which I'm very grateful," Pia said. "I wonder if he's too young to remember what happened."

His gold gaze flashed up to hers. "I hope he remembers everything. I hope it scared him. He's got dangerous abilities, and he going to grow up in a world full of enemies. He has to learn discipline early and to not go off by himself."

"That sounds so hard," she whispered.

"It *is* hard, but I have faith in him," Dragos said. "He may be small, but he's already proven that he has a big soul. He can handle it. And in the meantime, we'll put bars on his bedroom windows."

"I want them installed before we get home." She rubbed dry, tired eyes. The thought of him possibly getting loose outside the penthouse, so high off the ground, made her feel physically ill.

"They will be. I'll make the call in a few minutes."

"My lord." Hugh spoke hesitantly.

Both Pia and Dragos turned to the other man who knelt in front of him. Hugh's plain, bony face bore an anguished expression. As he opened his mouth to speak,

Dragos told him in a weary voice, "Just don't. It wasn't your fault. It wasn't Eva's fault."

"If anything, it was our fault," Pia said. "Liam's evolving so fast, we haven't seen in time all the implications of what that might mean. We have to start thinking faster and planning better."

Hugh didn't appear convinced, but at least he fell silent.

"Open up a bottle of wine," Dragos told him. "We've all earned a drink."

The other man's expression lightened somewhat, and he rose to his feet.

Dragos turned to Pia. He asked telepathically, *How are you doing?*

I'm tired. She looked down at Liam and stroked his back. *And so grateful. And you?*

The same. He paused. *Do you want to go home?*

Her head came up. *Hell, no. We are, by God, going to have our vacation. We had a really bad, bad day, but it's over with now. They were dumb jerks, and I will not let them be that important. Unless, of course, you want to go home.*

He smiled. *Hell, no.*

She suddenly remembered and said out loud, "There's a motorboat floating around with a fortune in treasure on it."

"And more sitting on the ocean floor," Dragos added.

Hugh handed them each a glass of wine. Pia clinked her glass against Dragos. "You've got your work cut out for you tomorrow."

Epilogue

L iam slept for a very long time. When he woke up, he was cuddled in bed with Mommy under warm, soft covers. As he lifted his head, she said, "Good morning, my love. Did you sleep well?"

He nodded and looked at the empty space in the bed.

"Daddy has gone to find the boat we lost, and to collect some treasure. You and I are going to spend the day on the beach. Does that sound good to you?"

He nodded again.

She dressed in shorts and a tank top and took him to the kitchen. He shapeshifted into his dragon form and she fed him a delicious breakfast of tender, sautéed pork tenderloin, which he gobbled up. He watched with interest as she ate her breakfast of cantaloupe and blueberries, until she noticed his attention and offered him bites of fruit. He gobbled that up too.

She looked delighted. "You're not a carnivore. You're omnivorous."

After breakfast they went to the beach. The sun felt deliciously warm. Liam stayed in his dragon form, ignored his other toys, wrapped his forelegs around bunny and fell asleep. He napped and woke, and napped some more, while Mommy read and occasionally frowned at him. Once she asked, "Are you okay, Peanut?"

He nodded and yawned. He was just tired.

Later in the day, Liam rolled to his feet as a motorboat chugged up to the nearby pier. Daddy stood at the wheel, looking satisfied. Mommy scooped Liam up and walked down the pier. Daddy lifted them both into boat, and Liam stared with interest at the soggy suitcase and two metallic containers.

Daddy kissed Mommy. When it was Liam's turn, he lifted his head for his kiss.

"Did you get it all?" Mommy asked.

Daddy nodded. He threw open the suitcase and the containers.

A bolt of pure love hit Liam.

"Wow!" Mommy said. "We've sure got a lot of treasure."

"Wait a minute." Daddy sounded amused. "What do you mean 'we'? I thought this was my treasure."

"Technically, I don't think that's possible anymore." Mommy sounded smug. "We're mated, married, and as I just realized the other day, we have no prenup."

"You just realized that the other day, did you?" Daddy laughed.

Liam couldn't stand it any longer. He wriggled to get out of Mommy's arms. As she bent to let him go, he scrambled over to the suitcase as fast as he could and dove into the gold coins. Picking up one coin after the other, he stared at them in complete fascination. Feeling giddy, he rolled around on them.

These were the best toys ever.

Now both Mommy and Daddy were laughing as they watched him.

Daddy said, "I'm not sure either you or I own that treasure anymore."

Liam clutched as many coins as he could in both paws and hugged them to his chest as he gave his parents his best, sunniest smile.

About the Author

Thea Harrison resides in Colorado. She wrote her first book, a romance, when she was nineteen and had sixteen romances published under the name Amanda Carpenter.

She took a break from writing to collect a couple of graduate degrees and a grown child. Her graduate degrees are in Philanthropic Studies and Library Information Science, but her first love has always been writing fiction. She's back with her paranormal Elder Races series. You can check out her website at: www.theaharrison.com, and also follow her on Twitter @TheaHarrison and on Facebook at www.facebook.com/TheaHarrison. You can sign up for Thea's newsletter at http://theaharrison.com/contact-requests/.

Look for these titles from
Thea Harrison

THE ELDER RACES SERIES
Published by Berkley

Dragon Bound

Half-human and half-wyr, Pia Giovanni spent her life keeping a low profile among the wyrkind and avoiding the continuing conflict between them and their Dark Fae enemies. But after being blackmailed into stealing a coin from the hoard of a dragon, Pia finds herself targeted by one of the most powerful–and passionate—of the Elder Races.

As the most feared and respected of the wyrkind, Dragos Cuelebre cannot believe someone had the audacity to steal from him, much less succeed. And when he catches the thief, Dragos spares her life, claiming her as his own to further explore the desire they've ignited in one another.

Storm's Heart
Serpent's Kiss
Oracle's Moon
Lord's Fall
Kinked

ELDER RACES NOVELLAS
Published by Samhain Publishing

True Colors

Meeting your soulmate? Great. Preventing your possible murder? Even better.

Alice Clark, a Wyr and schoolteacher, has had two friends murdered in as many days, and she's just found the body of a third. She arrives at the scene only minutes before Gideon Riehl, a wolf Wyr and current detective in the Wyr Division of Violent Crime—and, as Alice oh-so-inconveniently recognizes at first sight, her mate.

But the sudden connection Riehl and Alice feel is complicated when the murders are linked to a serial killer who last struck seven years ago, killing seven people in seven days. They have just one night before the killer strikes again.

And every sign points to Alice as the next victim.

Natural Evil
Devil's Gate
Hunter's Season

AMANDA CARPENTER ROMANCES
Published by Samhain Publishing

A Deeper Dimension
The Wall
A Damaged Trust
The Great Escape
Flashback

OTHER WORKS BY THEA HARRISON

Dragos Takes a Holiday

7910077R00072

Made in the USA
San Bernardino, CA
23 January 2014